The Ice Between Us

An Off-Limits Opposites Attract Sports
Romance

Clara Bridges

LPS Publishing House LLC

Contents

Chapter 1

Jenna

I don't look back when I close the apartment door for the last time. I don't trust myself too.

The hallway smells like it always has—like burnt toast, old carpet, and the weird lavender air freshener my neighbor sprays directly into the vent system. The scent usually hit me with a dull ache of familiarity, a bland comfort in the chaos, but today it just felt... thin. Like a memory worn transparent.

My suitcase wheels stick on the worn patch of linoleum outside apartment 2B, right where they always do, like the building itself is trying to make me stay. And for once, a part of me felt a tug of resentment at the resistance, a whisper of what-if that I immediately pushed down.

Mr. Costas watches me from his office-slash-living room down the hall, one elbow resting on the window unit that wheezes year-round like it's doing the Lord's work. He doesn't say anything at first. Just sips his coffee and scratches the patchy side of his beard.

"Left a gouge in the wall when you moved the bookshelves," he finally says.

I nod, gripping the handle of my suitcase tighter. "You can keep the deposit." The words were clipped, automatic. A small price to pay for escape, for the chance to erase the imprint of a life I'd tried, and failed, to build here. The gouge wasn't just in the wall; it felt like it was in me, a raw, unhealing divot of past mistakes.

He snorts like that was a foregone conclusion anyway. "You leave anything behind?"

"Just a cracked lamp and a year I can't get back."

That earns a blink. Maybe even a flicker of sympathy. But it's gone as quickly as it appears, replaced with the same disinterested shrug I've come to expect. "Keys."

I set them on the crooked little side table next to the mail bin, where someone's past-due electricity notice lies open like a warning.

For a second, I hesitate. It's not the apartment I'll miss or the peeling paint along with the unreliable heat and a bathroom window that never quite closed. It's the version of me that once believed this place could be the start of something. That I could build a life here with nothing but my sketchpad, a laptop, and a half-formed dream.

I step into the hall, suitcase trailing behind me like dead weight, and head down the stairs with my chin high and my throat tight.

Outside, the air is thick with that late summer humidity that makes everything feel like it's been dipped in sweat and regret. I load the last of my boxes into the backseat of my rusted sedan and close the trunk with both hands one to shut it, the other to keep it from bouncing back open again.

My phone vibrates in the cupholder. A text from a number I should have blocked by now.

"You sure this is what you want?"

I don't answer. I just stare at the screen until it fades to black, like even the phone is tired of asking.

Sliding into the driver's seat, I take one last glance at the building. The windows are dark. No one's come outside to say goodbye. I shouldn't be surprised.

No one in that life ever really saw me. Not fully.

So, I turn the key and the engine grumbles to life. The old GPS suctioned to the dashboard lights up, its cheerful voice announcing a seven-hour drive north like it's a spa weekend.

"Next stop, Willow Cove," I mutter, pulling onto the street. "Population: probably suspicious of outsiders and definitely too small for me to disappear in."

Rain starts somewhere around hour four. Soft at first and just enough mist gathering on the windshield. But it thickens as I turn off the highway and onto a winding two-lane road flanked by woods so dense they look painted on.

By the time I see the carved wooden sign that says Welcome to Willow Cove – Where the Lake Mends What Life Breaks, the clouds have opened up entirely, and the wipers are losing the battle.

I grip the wheel a little tighter. Part of me wants to turn around and go back. But there's nowhere left to go back to.

I merge onto the highway somewhere just north of the city, windshield streaked with rain and the weight of everything I didn't say pressing into my chest like a seatbelt pulled too tight.

The radio is on low with an indie folk station I used to put on during long nights of freelance projects and muted crying jags. Right now, a woman with a voice like honey through gravel is singing about leaving behind a house that never felt like home. It figures. Even the music has better timing than I do.

Outside, the landscape starts to unravel. Strip malls fade into chain restaurants. Chain restaurants give way to empty parking lots, then long stretches of farmland and forests that go on for miles, interrupted only by the occasional rusted gas station or crumbling billboard offering "homestyle pie" or "last clean bathroom for 60 miles."

The city loosens its grip slowly, reluctantly, like a bad relationship that still thinks it has a chance.

I pass a broken-down barn sagging under its own history, a field of sunflowers bent from last night's storm, and a single kid standing in a gravel driveway, arms outstretched to catch the rain like it's falling just for her.

The farther I go, the more the noise inside me changes. It isn't quiet, exactly. But it shifts from panic to something closer to ache. A hollow kind of hope.

I glance at the dash. Four more hours.

The GPS chirps out its directions like it believes in me. "Turn left onto County Road 18 in two miles." Like it's that simple. Like a new direction is all it takes to rewrite a life.

I adjust the heat even though I'm not cold. My fingers tap the steering wheel to the rhythm of the music, half on autopilot, half holding onto the song like a lifeline. It's the first time I've let myself be still in weeks.

Every so often I spot signs for towns I've never heard of the places with names like Maple Hollow and Sparrow's End. Places where people probably leave their keys in the ignition and bake casseroles for new neighbors.

And then there's Willow Cove.

Callie had described it like a secret worth keeping. "It's a town you run to when the world breaks you," she said over a staticky call from a Paris café. "Where the lake knows things and where people heal whether they want to or not."

At the time, I thought she was just being poetic.

But as the road narrows and the trees lean in like they're whispering to one another, I start to wonder if maybe she meant it.

The suns already slipped behind a shelf of low, pewter clouds by the time the fuel light dings on. It's not loud, just one soft blink and an orange glow on the dash. But it punches a hole straight through my already-tight chest.

"Seriously?" I flick the gauge. It doesn't move. I could've sworn I filled up before leaving the city. Then again, it's been a long day and an even longer week and apparently, denial burns faster than gasoline.

I slow to a crawl as the trees thicken, crowding the two-lane road like they've been waiting to close in. Just as my nerves begin to coil, I catch sight of a weathered gas station sign up ahead, tucked beneath a canopy of branches. The kind you'd miss if you blinked.

It's not promising. More like... something out of an old road trip horror movie that cuts to static right before the jump scare.

Still, I take the turn.

The gravel crunches under my tires as I ease into the lot. One crooked pump. A narrow storefront with yellowed windows. The plastic letters on the marquee overhead are sun-faded and half gone. It reads: W L OW G S — ICE. B IAT C ER. SODA.

I choose to believe it once said *Willow Gas – Ice. Bait Cooler. Soda.* I hope.

I park beside the pump, eyeing the mechanism. There's no card reader—just a faded sign in Sharpie that reads PAY FIRST IN-SIDE taped over a cracked display screen. Of course.

Inside, the station smells like bacon grease, old coffee, and something faintly metallic like dust on a radiator. A radio plays low in the background, all static and seventies guitar riffs. Behind the counter sits a man in a moss-green trucker hat, flipping through a battered Reader's Digest.

He glances up, then back down. "Pump still works. Mostly. Gotta jiggle it."

"Good to know," I say, digging through my bag for cash. "I'm not from around here."

He eyes me again. Slower this time. "Figured. You've got city shoulders."

"City... shoulders?"

"Too tight." He waves vaguely in my direction. "It takes about three months for 'em to drop. Six, if you're stubborn."

I offer a tired smile, hand him a twenty. "I guess we'll find out what kind I am."

He grunts something like approval and slides the drawer shut. "Pump'll stop when it's full. Don't fight it. It wins."

Outside, the air is heavy but still. Not quite muggy just... hushed. Like the world's holding its breath. A hawk circles high above the treetops, then vanishes.

I hook the nozzle and let it run, propping my hip against the car. In the distance, the road stretches empty in both directions, no sign of anyone coming or going. My reflection catches faintly in the car window: smeared eyeliner, a stubborn curl sticking up, eyes that look too tired for twenty-nine.

I hate how visible it all is. How lost looks like something you wear.

When the pump finally clicks, I slide the nozzle back into place, cap it off, and climb back into the driver's seat.

Back on the road, the forest leans closer. The GPS calmly announces my next turn. Two hours to Willow Cove.

I don't know what I'll find when I get there. But whatever it is... it has to be better than what I left behind.

I slide back into the car, slam the door shut a little harder than necessary, and start the engine.

Or try to.

Instead, it clicked and died. The dashboard lights flickered for a brief moment, then went black as the rain filled sky.

My stomach drops. "Oh, come on. Not now."

I twist the key again. Same thing. The car coughs, then falls silent.

For a second, I just sit there. Palms flat on the steering wheel. Forehead resting between them. As if sheer willpower might jumpstart the engine or the life, I'm trying so hard to outrun.

With a slow breath and a curse, I swallow before it makes it out of my mouth, I pop the hood and climb out.

The air has shifted. It's still warm, still heavy, but quieter now. Like the woods around the station are listening in.

I walk back inside the station, trying to smooth the nerves in my voice. "Hey, uh... sorry, weird question. You wouldn't happen to know anything about engines that click but don't start?"

The attendant looks up, unsurprised. "Yours?"

"Yeah."

He sighs, unfolds himself from his stool, and grabs a rag that's seen better centuries. "Let's take a look."

Outside, he props open the hood, pokes around like a man who's seen this a dozen times before, and mutters to himself.

"Battery's hanging on by a thread. Could be the starter, too." He taps something metallic. "You heading far?"

"Willow Cove."

That earns a faint grunt. "Ah. Up by the lake."

He straightens and wipes his hands. "Try it now."

I slip behind the wheel, twist the key again. The engine sputters, then grudgingly roars to life like it had to think about it first. Relief floods my chest.

He taps the roof. "She's running, but you've probably got a week—maybe two—before something gives. Cold weather'll finish her off."

"Great." I smile tightly. "Can't wait."

He glances at the cloudy sky. "Looks like you're chasing weather too. Wouldn't linger on these back roads. They get weird once the sun drops."

"Noted."

He heads back inside, leaving me alone with the hum of the engine and that unsettled feeling that's been growing since the city faded behind me.

The car is running. The road is open. The map is clear. And yet my hands shake just slightly on the wheel as I pull back onto the road

I tell myself it's just nerves or my exhaustion or maybe it's just the car.

But deep down, I know better. Something is shifting. I can feel it. And Willow Cove is closer with every mile.

The first drop hits like a warning.

Then another. Then a dozen more, splattering across the windshield in lazy, heavy taps. It's as if the clouds are testing their weight before they finally let go.

And when they do, they don't hold back.

Within seconds, I'm driving through a wall of water. The sound is deafening almost like someone turned the world into a drum and forgot to stop beating. The wipers groan across the glass, trying their best, but visibility narrows too almost nothing. The road becomes a slick ribbon, the edges swallowed by mist and rain pooling in low, reflective patches that look just shallow enough to be dangerous.

"Okay, okay, you're fine," I whisper to myself, tightening both hands on the wheel.

The trees on either side blur into dark, moving shadows, like the forest is closing in, erasing the horizon. My heart starts to pound in my ears; not from speed, but from the creeping sense that I can't quite tell where the road ends and the rest of the world begins.

A sharp gust of wind rocks the car just enough to make me gasp. I let off the gas, inching forward like the pavement could disappear beneath me at any second.

It's then, of course, that my favorite song starts playing.

A bittersweet guitar strum. A female voice I know like my own thoughts.

"If I lose the map, would you still find me...?"

My throat tightens. I know the words. I sing them anyway quietly at first, then louder. "Every wrong turn brought me closer to you..."

It feels foolish and brave, singing into this storm, but I need something to ground me. To keep me from unraveling.

The rain responds by pounding harder, like it's trying to drown the music out completely.

Then the station cuts too static.

I flinch.

"This is Vermont Public Weather Service with an urgent regional update—"

A male voice comes through, tinny and calm in a way that feels wildly inappropriate given the contents of the message.

"A flash flood warning is now in effect for all of Larkspur County, including the Silverpine Lake region and the town of Willow Cove."

My eyes flick to the GPS. Still blinking, still directing me forward.

"Flooding has been reported on rural roads between Maple Hollow and Pine Hollow Ridge. Mudslides possible in lower elevation zones. Motorists are advised to avoid unnecessary travel."

A warning chime sounds from the dashboard and another drop in the bucket of bad timing.

My hands are clammy against the steering wheel. The car fishtails ever so slightly as I round a slow curve, and I let out a breath I didn't know I was holding.

The road is no longer a road, it's a suggestion, blurred and wet and winding toward a town I've never seen, in a car that might not survive the next hill.

The storm is relentless now. Rain runs in sheets down the windows, turning the outside world into a kaleidoscope of movement and shadows. It feels like being inside a washing machine. Every fiber of my sweater clings to my skin, damp from the creeping leak under the window seal. My left foot is cold. The floor mat is soaked.

I want to cry. But it would only fog the windshield worse.

"Just get there," I whisper. "One mile at a time. Just get there."

The GPS speaks again, oblivious. "Turn right in 0.3 miles."

Lightning flashes, illuminating a wooden road sign that flickers into view as it's warped and half-covered in moss.

Welcome to Willow Cove.

And just like that, I realize I'm not just driving through a storm.

I'm driving straight into it.

The turn comes suddenly—almost too late. The tires skid slightly as I ease off the slick main road and onto a narrow, tree-lined path that winds like a secret. It's not paved. Gravel pings the underside of the car, kicking up mud and broken leaves with every cautious inch forward.

Branches arch overhead, dripping from the storm, their weight sagging low enough to kiss the roof of the car. The GPS goes quiet. No more instructions. Just a thin blue line on the screen leading deeper into the woods and toward whatever waits at the end.

I slow even more as the trees break.

And then I can start to see small parts of the town itself.

Just a single lane of houses nestled close like old friends keeping each other warm. Wooden porches with chipping paint. Window boxes spilling over with rain-soaked flowers with a white steeple rising modestly above the trees in the distance. Everything's still, like the storm paused time itself.

The air shifts the second I cross the invisible line into town. It's thicker. Heavier with scents mixed of wet cedar, wood smoke, and something almost sweet, like cinnamon and old books.

I blink back the sudden sting in my eyes. It's not beautiful, exactly. It's honest.

Like the kind of place that doesn't need to impress you. The kind of place that lets you come undone in peace.

I spot the lake through a break in the trees it's Silverpine, Callie had said. It stretches out behind the town, half-shrouded in mist, its surface rippling gently despite the storm. Like it's breathing.

The rain's softened to a cold drizzle now, just enough to make everything shimmer.

My shoulders ache from tension I didn't realize I was holding.

I turn onto a narrow lane, the gravel crunching softer here, and follow Callie's directions one more time.

Left at the stone wall. Right past the mailbox with the cardinal flag. Fourth house on the right—the one with the blue shutters and wind chimes.

The car crests the hill slowly, like it's holding its breath right alongside me.

And then—there it is. Nestled between two towering sugar maples and half-hidden behind a weathered split-rail fence is Callie's cottage.

The driveway curves inward gently, winding like a ribbon through a carpet of damp leaves and wild grass, the edges blurred by weeks of soft rain and soft neglect. The house itself is every inch as whimsical as the photos with the white clapboard siding, navy blue shutters, and a wide, wraparound porch with string lights woven through the banister like it's always half-prepared for a celebration.

A wind chime tinkles faintly in the breeze, and I can just make out the flicker of warm porch light against the early dusk. It's the kind of glow that says come in, dry off, you made it.

My throat tightens unexpectedly.

I ease the car around the curve, the tires crunching on gravel as the cottage unfolds fully into view. A rain-slick birdbath leans to one side. Ferns crowd the steps. One of the window boxes is overflowing, half wild, half whimsical. It's the sort of place that feels like it's been waiting for someone to return too even if they never lived there in the first place.

Something inside me cracks open just a little.

I made it. I really made it when all of a sudden,

The engine lurches with a loud, unnatural jolt. The dashboard flashes a brief warning light and I don't have time to read it before the entire car shudders beneath me.

"No, no, no—don't you dare."

It does.

With a final, stubborn cough, the engine dies completely. Silence drops like a stone.

I coast the last few feet up the driveway, hands clenched on the wheel, until the car rolls to a dead stop halfway between the porch and the overgrown hydrangeas.

Outside, the wind stirs the chimes again.

Inside, I let my forehead drop to the steering wheel and close my eyes.

So close.

I take a deep breath, grip the door handle, and push it open. It sticks, of course. Then bursts outward like it's had enough of me too.

The cold hits first it's sharper now that the storm's passed, like the air is rinsed clean but still angry. The wind snatches my hood and tugs hair into my mouth. I spit it out with a muttered groan and step onto the gravel... except it's not gravel anymore.

It's mud. Thick, wet, deceptively deep.

My boot sinks immediately, ankle-deep. I stagger, grabbing the edge of the door for balance, but it's too late. A cold, wet slosh seeps in over the top of my sock, and I let out a strangled sound halfway between a shriek and a sob.

I pop the trunk, praying my luggage has held up. The hinge groans like it's judging me, and the trunk door slaps upward as I grab the handle of my suitcase—

Too fast. Too hard.

The entire thing launches out like it's been lying in wait, bounces off the bumper, and lands squarely in a mud puddle the size of a kiddie pool.

"NO—no, no, no!"

The zipper bursts. Like actually bursts. Half of my life explodes onto the ground in a soggy avalanche of socks, sweaters, and a very personal lace bralette I hadn't even worn yet.

I scramble forward, slipping, sliding, grabbing at items like I'm chasing down a flock of startled birds.

A makeup bag splashes open, foundation seeping like a crime scene. My favorite sketchbook hits the mud, pages curling the moment they touch water. A boot rolls into the underbrush like it's making a break for it.

I drop to my knees with a choked breath, shivering, hair in my face, hands covered in cold, wet leaves and worse.

This is not a meet-cute. This is not a charming small-town arrival. This is a humiliation parade with front-row seats.

"Okay," I whisper, my voice shaking. "Okay. You're fine. Just... get it together."

But when I try to stand, one of my boots won't come unstuck from the mud. I lift my foot only for the boot to stay behind, suctioned in place like the ground itself doesn't want me here.

I nearly tip over.

And that's the moment I hear it; A low, unimpressed voice behind me and I freeze not realizing I had an audience.

"You planning to wrestle the whole driveway, or just the puddle?"

I am mid-grab; one hand still wrapped around a soaked sports bra.

Slowly, I straighten.

I am already on the edge: agitated, humiliated, and barely holding it together. I fling my wet hair back from my face in one aggressive swipe. It slaps against my neck like a soggy curtain as I turn toward the voice.

Slowly turn.

He's standing at the edge of the porch steps. Shirtless. Sweatpants. Broad-shouldered. Rainwater still clinging to the ends of his hair. And a face so carved and unbothered, it looks like it was designed in a lab to make women either swoon or swing a boot at him.

The tension in my chest spikes and then sharpens.

I don't swoon. Not today. Today I am cold, wet, and just done.

"And you are?" I snap, straightening, mud dripping from the edge of my sleeve.

"JP." He jerks his chin toward the porch. "Callie's brother."

Of course he is. The one she never mentioned would be home. The one I was definitely *not* supposed to meet while holding a lacy thong and looking like a swamp creature.

I grab a handful of soggy clothes and start stuffing them into my bag with messy, angry motions. "Great. You get to be the first local who witnesses my total breakdown. Welcome to the show."

He leans against the porch railing, arms crossed, expression unreadable.

"You always introduce yourself by cussing out your luggage?"

I glare at him. "Only when it betrays me."

He lifts one brow like he's not sure if I'm joking or unstable.

I finish shoving the last of my things back into the suitcase, which now zips halfway before catching on something inside. I force it. It whines. I don't care.

He doesn't offer to help either, in fact he doesn't even move at all.

The silence between us stretches out it's cold, rigid, and full of nope. It's not just awkward. It's something sharper. He's not smiling and I'm not apologizing.

And just like that, the air between us ices over.

I shove one last sweater that's mud-streaked and inside out into the now-bulging suitcase and drag the zipper closed with the kind of force usually reserved for tug-of-war competitions. It sticks halfway, and I yank it like it owes me money. It finally snaps shut with a sound that feels like a tiny victory in a day made entirely of defeats.

I grab the handle, lift the entire dripping mess of a bag, and stomp toward the porch like I'm three years old and someone just took my favorite crayon.

Every step squelches. My socks still soaked from earlier which makes that awful sloop noise with each stomp. The wheels on the suitcase are useless, caked in mud and protesting with each bounce against the warped steps. A bra strap dangles from the side like a white flag of surrender.

JP doesn't move.

Not when I hit the bottom stair. Not when I take the next two with the grace of a stomping goat. Not even when I nearly trip over the top one and mutter something under my breath that definitely isn't a thank you.

When I finally reach the porch, I don't pause. I don't look at him. I charge forward, clutching the suitcase like a protest sign right up until I realize we're about to collide.

He doesn't step aside.

Neither do I.

We stop just inches from each other, the porch boards groaning beneath us.

He's taller than I realized. Broader, too. Up close, he smells like soap mixed with rain and heat, like someone who wasn't the least bit rattled by the weather I just nearly drowned in. His jaw is sharp, stubbled, clenched. His eyes? Cold. A storm all on their own.

I lift my chin, refusing to be the first one to flinch.

"I'm guessing you're not the welcome committee," I snap.

His gaze drops to the suitcase, to the bra strap hanging off the side, then back to my face.

"Wasn't expecting guests today," he says, voice low, even, laced with something unreadable. "Especially ones who pick fights with puddles."

I suck in a sharp breath, lips parting with the kind of retort I'll regret later but I don't say it. Because I'm too tired. Too wet. And somehow, still too proud.

I shift the suitcase between us and force a tight smile. "Well. Surprise."

JP doesn't budge. Doesn't blink. Just slowly reaches into the pocket of his sweatpants and pulls out a key.

He holds it up between two fingers, casual as can be, and lets it dangle there they are just out of my reach. The metal catches the porch light, swinging ever so slightly like a baited hook.

I stare at it. Then at him. He raises one brow, deadpan. "Say please."

My jaw clenches. "Seriously?"

"You want to go inside or not?"

"Do you want to not get punched or not?"

He huffs it might've been a laugh if it weren't so dry and drops the key in my open palm. His fingers brush mine. They're warm. Unreasonably warm and that's when it hits me:

Callie's voice, in my head, like a warning she meant as a joke— "Don't fall for my brother. Seriously. He's got that quiet, broody thing that short-circuits your good judgment."

I grip the key tighter, like I'm holding something more dangerous than it looks.

"You're lucky I'm tired," I mutter, stepping past him.

"You're lucky Callie's the one who invited you," he says evenly. "Anyone else, and I'd have left you out there with the puddle you were yelling at."

I stop mid-step. Turn slowly.

"That puddle tried to steal my boot."

He just shrugs. "Maybe it was trying to tell you something."

We stand there, toe to toe again, breath clouding between us in the cooling air.

"I don't know what Callie told you," I say, voice low, controlled, "but I'm not here to make trouble."

His gaze holds mine. Steady. Cold. "Then maybe try not arriving like a hurricane next time."

My heart kicks once, then hardens.

I grip the key, step inside, and shoulder the suitcase over the threshold. The cottage smells like cinnamon, lemon wood polish, and something soft I can't name. I don't let myself take it in.

Not yet.

I pause just long enough to look over my shoulder.

JP stands on the porch, watching. Expression unreadable his arms crossed again and his guard firmly in place.

I meet his eyes. "You might want to move your storm shelter. Looks like trouble's staying a while."

Then I slam the door behind me.

Chapter 2

JP

The door slams so hard, one of the wind chimes lets out a startled clatter. I stare at it for a second, then let out a slow breath through my nose.

So.

She's here.

I turn away from Callie's porch and walk back down the gravel path toward my own place. It's only twenty feet away and a world apart.

My house sits lower on the slope, tucked behind a row of sugar maples with leaves already starting to blush with early fall. The paint's still in decent shape it's soft gray with charcoal trim but everything about the place feels... muted. Intact, but untouched. Like someone pressed pause halfway through living here and forgot to hit play again.

No porch swing. No lights strung along the eaves. Just a straight-lined front step, a rain-darkened welcome mat, and a screen door that sticks if you don't pull it just right.

Where Callie's place is overgrown and buzzing with life from wind chimes, potted herbs, cracked garden gnomes where mine is stripped down to essentials. Trimmed hedges. Closed blinds. A porch light that I keep turned off even when I'm home.

There's a patch of grass along the side where I used to think about building a fire pit just never did it.

The only thing I've added since moving back is the punching bag hanging from the beam in the carport. It's swaying a little now in the wind, like even it's restless.

I jog up the short path, the gravel crunching under my steps in a rhythm that used to come easy before everything changed. The house rises ahead, quiet and square against the trees, its familiar silhouette offering no comfort, just routine. But as soon as my foot hits the first step, pain shoots through my knee with the sharp, unforgiving clarity of a blade catching just beneath the bone.

It stops me cold.

The kind of pain that doesn't throb or swell it strikes fast and deep, a reminder that no matter how many days I pretend otherwise, my body still remembers the break. My hand grips the railing out of instinct, not weakness, though sometimes those feel like the same thing now. The step beneath me groans, or maybe that's just me, breathing harder than I should have to, caught between reflex and refusal.

I close my eyes for half a second, but it's already enough to take me back.

The lights overhead. The sound of skates scraping to a halt. The weight of silence after the crowd gasped as one, realizing something had gone horribly wrong. The cold of the ice pressing into my back as I lay there, leg twisted out of alignment with the rest of me, and the nauseating certainty blooming in my chest before the trainers even reached me.

It wasn't just the knee. It was what came with it.

The end of something I didn't know how to live without.

There was no drama to it, no final game with a jersey-throw or handshake line. Just a sharp pain, a stretcher, and the slow unraveling of a future I'd wrapped everything around. I didn't cry when they told me. I didn't ask questions. I nodded, like a man being sentenced who already knew the verdict. After that, it was all physical therapy and polite condolences, people telling me how "lucky" I was to be walking again, how I could coach, how life could go on.

But they don't tell you how to walk back into the town you left behind, the one that only knew you as the kid with skates laced tighter than his future. They don't prepare you for the hollow version of yourself that returns.

I open my eyes. The pain lingers, but it's more memory now than threat. I shift my weight carefully, forcing the knee to hold me as I climb the remaining steps, slow and deliberate, because that's how you have to move when the dream you spent a lifetime building has collapsed under you.

The porch light clicks on as I reach the top, flooding the entry-way in that cold, motion-activated glow. I don't bother looking back at Callie's cottage. I can still feel the tension in the air like static between storm systems.

I open the door to my own place and step inside, letting the quiet settle around me like dust in an undisturbed room.

There are no photos on the walls. No echoes of who I was before the break. Just clean surfaces, empty spaces, and the unspoken truth that I haven't really moved in like I've just been occupying square footage.

I shut the door behind me and exhale, slow and steady.

The pain may fade but the regret doesn't.

The silence inside stretches too long.

I lean against the kitchen counter, the same one I've leaned on every night since coming back, and stare at the cabinets like they might rearrange themselves into something worth staying for. The fridge hums while the clock ticks. The house offers nothing but air that's been still for far too long.

I need to move. Not just because the pain is creeping again, not just because the memory is louder tonight, but because if I stay in this house one minute longer, I'll start pulling apart things that don't need breaking.

I head down the hall, flick on the bedroom light, and grab the black quarter-zip hoodie from the back of the chair where I left it this morning. It's soft from years of wear, sleeves slightly stretched, but it fits better than anything else I own. I pull it on over my head, the familiar fabric brushing across the healing scar that still aches when the weather turns.

A T-shirt underneath, with washed worn in jeans and my work boots by the door.

Armor. Simple, forgettable, just enough to pass.

I grab my keys and wallet, shoulder into the jacket, and step outside without letting myself hesitate. The air hits cool against my skin, sharp and damp, but at least it's real. It smells like pine, wet gravel, and old earth like something trying to start over.

By the time I reach the truck, I already know where I'm headed.

The Willow Bean.

Not because I want company. Because I need noise, the heat with familiar walls that don't echo.

The bell over the café door chimes with that familiar soft ring, the kind that doesn't just announce your arrival it quietly reminds the room that you're back. That you haven't vanished, not entirely. The warmth inside hits me first with thick, welcoming, spiced cinnamon and coffee and something citrusy from the bakery case.

It smells the same as it always has. Like home, if home had ever felt like it could hold me.

A few heads lift from booths and coffee mugs, offering the kind of quick nods you only get in towns like this the acknowledgment without expectation. The way people greet someone they've known too long to make a fuss over, but not long enough to forget what they used to be.

I don't respond not much but just enough. The way you do when you don't want to linger in the past people still see on your face.

Miss Edie is already at the counter, eyes narrowing on me like she's checking for damage.

"Well," she says, her voice sweet as the butter she melts into her scones, "if it isn't my favorite emotionally unavailable regular. You here for caffeine or absolution?"

"Just coffee," I mutter, dragging a hand over the back of my neck, trying to brush off the cold that's clung to me all day, even after the rain stopped.

"Mm-hmm." She grabs a mug, pours with one hand like she's been doing it since the Civil War, and slides it toward me without another word. She knows better than to push. But she still pokes, in that gentle, needlepoint way of hers. "Table or to-go?"

I glance around the café and that's when I see her, in the far corner.

Soft chair by the fireplace her legs tucked up under her like she owns the space without trying. Her hair still damp at the ends. A charcoal pencil in one hand, a half-full mug in the other. Her sketchbook is open across her lap, pages tilted toward the low afternoon light, and she's humming a melody I can't quite place, low and easy, like she forgot the world is watching.

She doesn't see me.

But her presence pulses across the room like heat from a furnace someone else turned on.

And suddenly the café feels too warm. Too tight in the chest.

Miss Edie follows my gaze, and without missing a beat, glances toward the pastry case like she didn't just take a snapshot of every emotion on my face.

"That one's got weight to her," she says, voice low. "Storm in the bones. You feel it before you hear it."

"She's staying at my sister's," I reply flatly, like that should be warning enough.

Edie just hums, already loading a saucer with one of the cinnamon scones she knows I like but never ask for.

"She's temporary," I add.

"Most storms are."

She passes the saucer across the counter. "Go sit down. Try not to glower."

I take the coffee and the plate and choose the table in the far corner, just shy of Jenna's line of sight. Not because I'm hiding. Because I'm not hiding. At least that's what I tell myself.

Her voice floats over a moment later it's light, amused, woven with thank-you's and curiosity. She's talking to Miss Edie now, a few paces behind me, and the sound of her laughter slips into the cracks I didn't think this town still had the nerve to reach.

"Chamomile and lemon," Edie says brightly. "You look like someone who needs soft edges today."

Jenna laughs, surprised. "How do you know?"

Edie's response is laced with a smile. "I've been serving coffee longer than you've been forming opinions. I know a thunder-cloud when I see one."

Another soft laugh. Another pinprick under the skin.

And then the silence. Just long enough to know she's watching me now.

I don't turn. Just hold my cup steady, eyes on the knot in the wood grain beneath my thumb.

Miss Edie walks past me a moment later, carrying a tea towel over one shoulder and the scent of bergamot on her sweater. She stops beside my table, just long enough to lean in without looking at me directly.

"You're gonna have to speak to her eventually," she says, smoothing the corner of the napkin on my saucer. "You live next door, not in Antarctica."

"Antarctica sounds easier."

She gives a quiet laugh it's short, knowing, a sound that says she's seen this movie before and already knows how it ends.

Then, softer, slower with words she means to stick

"Even quiet men need a spark, JP."

She walks away without another glance.

And I sit there my hands still around a warm mug, tension tight in my shoulders, staring across the café at a woman I don't know, who doesn't know me, and yet somehow already feels like she's standing on the frozen bridge between the man I am and the one I used to be.

I don't finish the coffee. The scone sits untouched beside the napkin I never unfolded. I'm not hungry, and truthfully, I'm not sure I could keep anything down with the way the air in this room is wired tight between us.

I slide the mug back toward the center of the table, stand, and make my way to the counter. It's instinct more than decision like a habit, maybe. Movement as a form of escape.

Miss Edie meets me with a quiet sort of patience that feels both earned and dangerous. Her hands are already folded, her eyes soft but sharp, like she's watching me write a letter I won't sign.

"You need anything else, hon?"

I glance down toward the ice tea station without answering. Then, before I can stop myself and before I have the chance to weigh in whether this is smart or stupid, I gesture toward the drink Jenna ordered earlier.

"That lemon ginger tea she had," I say, voice low. "To go."

Edie's eyebrows lift just slightly, but she doesn't ask. Doesn't comment. Just turns and begins preparing it, her movements smooth and precise, as if this kind of request doesn't register as unusual in the rhythm of her day.

And that's when I do something even, I don't quite understand.

My hand moves without permission toward the small wire basket beside the counter it's one of those impulse shelves stocked with notebooks, pens, packs of local postcards. I grab the top item before I can change my mind.

It's a tiny spiral sketchpad, bright pink, the kind that looks like it should belong to a twelve-year-old with glitter pens and a sticker habit. The cover's stamped with a faded star, and the paper inside is thin, cheap but functional.

I place it beside the tea.

Edie pauses, then glances at the notebook. Then at me.

"You sure about that one?" she asks, the question light but weighted.

I hesitate for a beat too long. "She had a sketchbook, It was ruined and this just... seemed like a replacement."

She watches me closely, her expression unreadable, and wraps both items in quiet efficiency. She adds a honey stick and a small napkin, tucking them into the bag like she's blessing them.

"You want to leave it with me?" she asks gently. "Or are you planning to walk straight into the lion's den?"

I take the bag from her hands. "Don't make it sound so dramatic."

"Oh, honey," she says with a smile that's pure trouble. "It's already dramatic. You just haven't caught up yet."

I murmur a thank you and head toward the door but not before I pause beside Jenna's table. She hasn't looked up, but she knows I'm there. The tension in her shoulders tells me as much.

Without a word, I set the bag on the corner of her table, careful not to get too close. My hand stays in the air a second too long. Then I barely nod and step back.

She finally looks up.

And the second her eyes find the notebook inside the bag, her expression shifts first to confusion, then to something harder, sharper.

"Seriously?" she says, lifting the edge of the pink sketchpad like it might bite her. "Is this supposed to be cute?"

I stop, halfway to the door. "It's paper. I thought you'd prefer it over the muddy leaves you were sketching on earlier."

"Is this a joke to you?" she fires back, voice rising slightly, all sharp corners now. "Because this looks like something you'd give to a kindergartener who can't color inside the lines."

I turn slowly, but not all the way. "If I wanted to make a joke, you'd know. I was trying to help."

She scoffs. "Right, because nothing says 'supportive' like a hot tea and a notebook that looks like it came from a dollar store clearance bin."

The words shouldn't sting, but they do.

I exhale slowly, jaw tight, eyes fixed on the door like it's the only safe direction left to look.

"If you don't want it, throw it out," I say quietly.

Then I walk out slowly, deliberate and my shoulders squared like I'm not carrying her voice with me all the way to the truck.

Behind me, the bell chimes again, and just like that, the storm shifts directions.

Chapter 3

Jenna

The morning light creeps in like it's trying to be polite about it with soft, golden hues that are all apologetic through the slats of my blinds. But even sunlight feels like a personal attack when you've slept like garbage and your to-do list reads like a cry for help.

It warms the floor in perfect little rectangles, neat and golden across the scuffed hardwood, like even that has its life more together than I do. The smell of coffee still lingers from a half-finished mug I abandoned somewhere in the living room. I can't even remember if I drank it or just threatened to.

Outside, suburbia is having a moment. One of those mornings where everything looks like it was arranged by a wedding planner with too much time and too many Pinterest boards. Birds are practically harmonizing, lawnmowers hum in the distance, cheerful and well-behaved. A gentle breeze rustles the wind chimes next door in that peaceful, rhythmic way that says "this is where people who have matching sock drawers live."

And then there's my yard...

From the window, I can already see the grass curling over the edges of the walkway like it's trying to escape the property out of shame. One of the flowerbeds has fully given up, hosting what I hope is just last year's pumpkin vines and not some alien species slowly taking over. I've been meaning to pull the dead stuff out for... I don't know. A month? Two? I blink. It's June. So, three.

The HOA newsletter is probably already being drafted in blood-red ink.

But this morning, something in me snaps awake—not in a *motivated girlboss* kind of way, more like a fine, I'll do it myself mutter to the universe. I yank open the front door with the kind of resolve that doesn't last long but sure looks impressive at the start.

Cool air greets me first. Crisp, fragrant, stupidly lovely. It smells like fresh soil and lilacs and that impossible suburban calm that used to soothe me. Now it just reminds me of all the things I haven't figured out yet.

I step outside barefoot. The porch wood is still damp with early dew, the boards creaking a little like they're gossiping about me behind my back. I pause for a beat. Take it in. The sunlight dapples through the trees and glints off the hood of my neighbor's pristine minivan. Their grass is short. Their mulch is fresh. Their kids wear matching rain boots for no reason.

Across the street, someone is already pressure-washing their driveway. Just because. Just to feel something, probably.

I glance down at my own lawn. It's wild, defiant and one bad afternoon away from being declared a conservation zone and I sigh. This is fine, I can do this, I am going to do this.

Today is the day I pull myself together. Not emotionally. That ship sailed years ago and hit an iceberg of bad decisions. But physically? Logistically? Yes. I am going to mow this ridiculous lawn. I am going to fix the uneven spots along the fence line. I am going to pretend, for one solid hour, that I am the kind of person who thrives in the morning sun instead of squinting at it like it owes me money.

I down the rest of my cold coffee in one long, resigned gulp grimacing like it's a shot of cheap tequila and set the mug on the porch railing like some sort of suburban sacrificial offering.

"Alright," I mutter, stretching my arms overhead, trying not to focus on the weird crack my shoulder makes. "Let's mow some trauma."

I start toward the shed with all the confidence of someone who watched half a YouTube tutorial at 2 a.m. and believes in beginner's luck. The mower's in there. Probably angry. Probably held together with rust and spite.

But so am I.

Let's see which of us breaks first.

I tug open the warped shed door with both hands, gritting my teeth as it sticks like it always does in the lower corner swollen from some long-forgotten rainstorm and sheer homeowner denial. It groans open with the same dramatic flair I use when getting off the couch, revealing the dim, dusty cave of tools I don't fully understand and storage bins I haven't opened since I moved back.

Inside, it smells like sunbaked plastic, WD-40, and that specific brand of hopelessness that comes from inherited lawn equipment.

And there she is.

The mower.

All dented metal and silent judgment, crouched in the back like a sleeping dragon. I half expect it to hiss at me when I approach.

I swear it looks meaner than I remember, like it's aged into something more malevolent in its off-season. The handle leans to the left, and the wheels are caked with last year's regrets. I don't even check the gas tank. I'm not emotionally prepared for that kind of disappointment yet.

I squat beside it with my knees popping in protest and tug it forward, wincing as the wheels shriek against the wood floor.

"You and me," I whisper. "One job. Just one. Don't make this into a metaphor."

Dragging it out into the daylight feels like unveiling a crime scene. It catches on the doorframe. Twice. The right wheel nearly falls off. I have to tilt it awkwardly and mutter something about hating my life to get it over the threshold.

I manage to get it out to the lawn, place it like a crown jewel on a battlefield, and step back.

It looks… terrible. But not dead. Yet.

I bend to check the primer bulb, poking it three times like that's what you're supposed to do. I have no idea. I watched my uncle do it once while yelling at the Cowboys game. It seemed right then. It seems right now.

Then I grab the starter cord.

The handle is warm from the sun. My hand curls around it. My stance is decent. I take a breath, narrow my eyes, and pull.

Nothing.

A small, sad cough. A half-hearted puff of something. Then silence.

I yank again harder this time. The cord jerks, but the mower just groans like it wants me to give up and go back to therapy.

Third pull with more force, more faith, more sheer desperation and the mower coughs like a lifelong smoker waking up on a Monday.

Then it sputters again.

Then just as miraculously, triumphantly, defiantly it catches.

The engine rattles to life with a roar so loud it startles a flock of sparrows out of the neighbor's dogwood. A plume of gray smoke belches up in protest, but the sound holds. It's not elegant or even particularly healthy, but it's consistent. Choppy, ragged, slightly unhinged I think to myself it's just like me.

I freeze, blinking in shock, afraid to breathe too hard in case it dies again. For one long, absurd second, I just stand there, staring down at the mower like it's a newborn deer that just took its first wobbling steps.

"Oh my God," I whisper. "It's running."

The engine chugs along, shaking the metal frame like it's trying to rattle itself into an early retirement, but it's alive. Alive. After all these years. After all that neglect. This rusted-out hunk of betrayal has found its will to live and apparently, I'm the chosen one.

I straighten up, hands on my hips, grinning like I just solved a murder or won a pie contest in a town with exactly three eligible bachelors.

"I don't even need a man," I shout over the roar. "I have horsepower and trauma!"

The mower vibrates as if it disapproves of my feminism, but it stays running.

I bend, grip the handle, and shove.

And suddenly, we're in motion.

The mower lurches forward like a drunk shopping cart, chewing through the first patch of long grass with the grace of a buzz saw at a bridal shower. Blades spin. Grass flies. I barely keep it in a straight line, but the thing is working. Actually working.

One row down.

Then another.

The scent of fresh-cut grass rises thick into the air, all sharp green and childhood nostalgia, like summer vacations and front-porch lemonade. My calves are instantly flecked with clippings. There's a streak of dirt on my shin that I can't explain and don't have time to care about.

Because for once and just once something in my life is going exactly the way I want it to.

And the most unhinged part? It feels amazing.

I mow with the kind of determination usually reserved for sports montages and women running from their feelings. The hum of the engine swells beneath me like a battle cry. I'm slicing through weeds and chaos and possibly some very metaphorical overgrowth.

But somewhere around the third pass, the high starts to wear off.

My arms ache. My hair's stuck to the back of my neck. And of course, right on cue, my brain decides to offer up an unsolicited image of JP

The thought comes out of nowhere and lands like a rock in my shoe. Unavoidable. Unwelcome. Familiar.

"Stop it," I hiss, to no one and everyone.

I push harder.

Focus on the line. Focus on the grass. Focus on the way the mower chugs under my grip like a dependable, slightly concussed friend.

I hit a thick patch of clover and power through it with a growl, muttering something about emotional independence and carburetors. Sweat drips down my spine. I squint into the sunlight. My sandal catches on the edge of a tree root hidden in the grass and I stumble—not all the way down, but enough to throw off my line and nearly face-plant into the flowerbed.

I lurch, catch the handle at the last second, and hiss through my teeth.

"I am *fine*," I say, half to myself, half to the mower. "This is *totally normal behavior.*"

But I'm not fine.

I'm not fine at all.

Because this yard may be slowly coming under control.

But everything else?

Everything else is a mess I can't mow my way out of.

I'm halfway through the fourth pass, sweat prickling at my hairline, when the mower quits.

No warning. No coughing sputter. No noble mechanical death. Just a sharp click and then silence.

The blades stutter once before locking in place, and the engine goes dead like it's decided I'm not worth the effort anymore.

For a moment, I just stand there, my hands still wrapped around the handle, fingers clenched white as if I can will it back to life. My breath comes fast and shallow, too loud against the backdrop of sudden quiet. The breeze stirs the hem of my shirt, but I barely feel it. Every nerve in my body is coiled.

I press the primer and yank the cord again and to my surprise, nothing. Again I try harder this time and still nothing. A third pull now violent, frustrated and desperate. The mower doesn't even cough. It just sits there, smug and lifeless, like a dying star in a galaxy of my bad decisions.

"You've got to be kidding me," I mutter, voice trembling with rage I've been bottling up. "You had *one* job only one. I do everything else wrong this was supposed to be easy."

I slam my palm against the side of the engine, not to hurt it, but to keep from hurting something else. The plastic casing rattles. A screw clinks loose and falls into the grass, sealing its fate.

And mine.

I kick the back wheel—too hard this time—and immediately regret it. Pain shoots up my leg, sharp and immediate, but I'm too furious to care. I grab the starter cord and yank it one more time, purely out of spite.

Still. Dead.

"Unbelievable," I whisper, turning away, hands in my hair, elbows sharp and shaking. "Even this piece of junk knows when to give up."

"You know it's out of gas, right?"

The voice doesn't come from my memory.

It comes from behind me and not a figment of my imagination nor a real human sounding way too amused.

I spin around, jaw already tight, blood thudding behind my eyes.

A stranger stands at the edge of my property, one arm draped over the crooked top of the fence like he owns it. He must be in his late twenties, maybe. Broad shoulders beneath a rumpled hoodie and a backwards ball cap. Coffee in one hand and confidence in the other. He smiles like this is the beginning of something lighthearted.

It's not.

"Excuse me?" I ask, my voice clipped and cold enough to snap icicles off the roof.

He gestures with his coffee. "Probably just out of fuel. Mower's not broken, most likely just tired and thirsty. Like the rest of us."

"Do I know you?"

"Nope." He doesn't move. Doesn't flinch. "I was heading in to check on JP. Saw you out here going a few rounds with the lawn, figured I'd offer my unsolicited expertise."

My stomach knots. Of course he's one of his people.

Perfect.

"Well, thanks for the diagnosis," I say, stepping away from the mower, "but unless that coffee is gasoline, I don't really need help right now."

"You sure?" he asks. "Because from this side of the fence, it looks like you're one more pull away from setting it on fire."

"Maybe I am."

He grins, unfazed. "Fair warning, I'm not great in emergencies, but I'm excellent at documenting meltdowns. Want me to grab my phone?"

I blink at him, incredulous.

"Are you seriously standing there making jokes right now?"

"Would it help if I told you I make them at funerals too?"

I let out a short, humorless laugh. "God, you're exactly the kind of person this town breeds, aren't you?"

He gives a mock bow. "Benji Wilcox. Assistant coach at the rink. Certified chaos instigator. And at this moment? Your unsolicited mower therapist."

I cross my arms, heat rising up my throat. "And I'm the woman trying not to explode in front of a stranger while wrestling an outdated engine and unresolved trauma. So, unless you're here to pour gas or bury a body, maybe don't."

Benji shrugs, as easy as summer. "Can't help you with the first, but I've got a shovel in my truck."

I stare at him.

He grins wider.

And somewhere, beneath the burn of sweat and anger and humiliation, I feel something flicker: a pulse, a crack, the faintest outline of a laugh trying to break through.

But I press it down. Hard.

Because I'm not done being angry yet.

I don't dignify Benji's last comment with a response. I just turn on my heel and stalk across the yard like the grass personally insulted me.

The shed looms ahead, warped and sun-faded, its doors slightly ajar from earlier. I yank them open with more force than necessary, the left hinge groaning like it, too, resents being dragged into my drama. Inside, the space smells like damp wood, rust, and the ghosts of every abandoned project I thought I could handle on my own.

Somewhere beneath the cobwebbed shelves and cracked buckets, there's a dented red gas can. I know it. I've seen it. I may not have checked it before starting the mower, but I am not about to be out-patienced by a smug stranger with a perfect smile and a caffeine crutch.

I drop to my knees, start shifting aside a stack of brittle garden stakes, half a bag of expired fertilizer, and something unidentifiably plastic that crunches ominously.

Behind me, footsteps crunch in the grass.

I pause.

Of course.

Of course he followed me.

"Is this the part where you go full suburban vengeance and I end up buried under the raised beds?" Benji asks, leaning casually in the doorway, silhouetted against the sunlight like the world's most irritating action hero.

I don't look up. "This is the part where I find the gas can and prove I'm not completely incompetent."

"Hey, I never said you were. I said the mower was out of gas. The subtext was love."

I glare over my shoulder, crouched on the shed floor, one gloved hand inside a broken milk crate full of tangled bungee cords and resentment. "Do you always follow strangers into sheds?"

"Only the ones wielding garden tools with murder in their eyes."

I find the gas can wedged behind a sack of moldy potting soil and yank it free. The slosh inside confirms it's not empty. Vindication blooms in my chest like a flare.

I stand, turn toward him, and hold it up like a trophy. "See? Gas."

Benji claps once, slowly, like I just recited Hamlet. "Color me humbled."

"You should be," I mutter, brushing cobwebs off my knees and stepping past him.

He doesn't move. Just pivots slightly, walking backward as I storm toward the mower with the can clutched to my side like a weapon.

"You know," he says, easily keeping pace, "this whole act would be more convincing if you weren't clearly five seconds from yelling at your mower like it cheated on you."

"I'm five seconds from using it to mow you," I snap.

Benji laughs it's a full, unapologetic sound that chases me back into the open air and lands somewhere between charming and criminally annoying.

And I hate that I almost smile.

Almost.

I crouch low in the shed, hands sweeping through layers of brittle tools and warped plastic planters, each movement sharp and singular in its purpose. The air is stale and thick with the scent of damp wood and something metallic underneath maybe rust, maybe frustration turned tangible but I ignore it, narrowing my focus until my palm finds the familiar, scuffed edge of a gas can tucked behind a sagging bag of potting soil that feels like it's been fermenting for a decade. It takes effort to pry it free, the handle sticking slightly before releasing with a reluctant scrape that echoes louder than it should in the tight space.

I lift the can and tilt it gently. The weight is promising. The slosh inside confirms what I need, not a full tank, but enough. Enough to finish the job. Enough to win. Enough to put something, anything back in my control.

Rising slowly, my forearm brushes against the side of my jeans, leaving a smudge of dirt behind that I don't bother to acknowledge. As I turn toward the open doorway and find Benji still leaning there, the picture of amused patience, the curve of his mouth barely visible beneath the rim of his coffee cup. He doesn't speak, and thankfully, he doesn't try to follow me either, at least not yet.

I don't look at him for long. Don't offer a glare or a quip or even a sigh. Instead, I walk past him in silence, the gas can tight in her grip, my pace purposeful and clipped, my shoulders squared like armor. My arm brushes against his chest as I move through the narrow space between us it's intentional but not aggressive, not rude but solid enough to communicate everything I have no intention of saying aloud.

By the time I finally reach the mower, the sun has shifted higher in the sky, and the air is thicker, the grass beneath my shoes is warm and flattened from earlier passes. I kneeled beside the machine, uncaps the tank, and pour in the sloshy liquid. The scent of gasoline rises immediately it's raw and acrid and oddly satisfying, like progress distilled into something she can finally hold.

I don't check to see if Benji is still watching, though I have the feeling he is. I can feel the weight of his attention behind me, not leering or judging, just... present. It makes my pulse tick a little faster, not with embarrassment, but with something heavier. Sharper.

Once the tank is full, I set the can aside and grip the handle again, wrapping my fingers tightly around the starter cord with a steadiness that wasn't there ten minutes ago. The first pull is strong, not desperate or angry, just deliberate.

The mower sputters and rumbles. Then roars to life with a full-throated sound that feels, absurdly, like defiance.

I don't hesitate.

The moment it engages, I shove the machine forward with re-newed force, carving a fresh line into the thick grass that hadn't stood a chance from the beginning. My posture is rigid, mouth set in a line of determination that borders on dangerous, and the mower surges ahead beneath her grip like it knows not to question me anymore.

Each strip of the yard disappears in rhythmic, relentless rows. It doesn't feel rushed, but it doesn't slow either, and as I push forward past the dandelion patch, around the sagging fence post, toward the dogwood that's shedding petals like a lazy apology my expression doesn't shift, doesn't falter, doesn't soften.

This isn't yard work anymore.

This is reclamation.

Each pass is a declaration, not just to the mower or the yard or the man watching me from the edge of the fence, but to myself. A wordless, furious reminder that I haven't come undone, not really. That no matter how messy things look from the outside from the mud on my knees to the sweat down my back it's the emotional shrapnel still embedded from the name I refuse to say aloud, there is still something inside me that finishes what I starts.

And if Benji says anything behind me, I don't hear it. Or maybe I do, and simply doesn't care.

Because I don't turn around.

Let him watch.

Let the whole damn street watch.

This is mine now.

The yard, the silence, even the heat rising off my skin. The weight of everything that came before and the refusal to carry it the same way again. The fence, the mower, the mess. All of it.

My responsibility. My proof.

So, when I round the edge of the lawn near the back corner, I push too hard and don't slow down enough, my thoughts in ten paces ahead of my body, breath still ragged from the last surge of adrenaline. The left front wheel dips into a shallow rut, the one I stepped over a dozen times without fixing and the mower jerks violently sideways. I stumble, trying to catch it, but my shin hits the crossbar and my hands twist the handle as the machine leans into the old, weather-worn fence line.

The collision isn't loud, but it's decisive.

The mower clips the edge of the center post, and the wood reacts instantly, groaning under the pressure. The first crack is sharp, unexpected with a dry snap that makes the hair on her arms rise. Then the weight shifts, the support buckles, and the entire center panel folds forward like a house of cards that had been waiting for the right gust of wind.

The fence collapses with a resigned groan, breaking away from its foundation and landing with a dull crash into the neighbor's rosemary bush, sending up a cloud of brittle needles and splinters.

And just like that, the mower gives up too.

It sputters and coughs then on que it dies beneath my hands, the engine grinding to a halt with a finality that feels almost smug.

I just stand there, frozen, one hand still clutching the handle, body humming with shock and heat and something else I don't have the vocabulary for. My breath stutters once. Then again. I manage to look down at the mangled fence, the exposed posts, the raw wood where paint used to be.

I take a look at the mower all crooked in the grass, as lifeless as the apology no one ever gave me.

For a full five seconds, the world holds its breath.

Then I move.

Not slowly, not dramatically just with purpose. I'm controlled and cold.

As I step to the side, bracing my foot on the deck, and grab the starter cord like it insulted my family name. My fingers curl tightly; palm hot and slick, jaw locked with enough pressure to crack bone. I yank hard.

Nothing.

No rumble. No cough. Just silence and mechanical resistance.

I inhale through my nose, sharp and clean, like I'm about to dive underwater.

Then pull again harder this time, with all the weight of my shoulders behind it.

The mower sputters. Stutters. Then roars to life again, louder than before, angry and raw, as if it finally understands who it's dealing with.

I don't even hesitate. I don't give myself a moment to process or recover or speak. I just drive it forward without ceremony, slicing through the next row of overgrown grass like it's something personal, something that needs to be punished.

Each step is forceful, grounded, decisive. The blades chew through dandelions, crabgrass, the remains of her patience. Grass spits out in sprays, catching on my shins, sticking to the sweat on my arms, but I don't break stride. I keep moving, with my spine straight and hands steady, the sound of the engine drowning out every thought that's been clawing at my chest since the morning began.

I don't look over at the fence again.

I don't look at the mower.

I don't even look at Benji, who remains where I left him, leaning against the far post with his hoodie sleeves pushed up and his coffee cup loose in his grip, watching me with a stillness I haven't earned and not ready to accept.

He doesn't speak.

He doesn't laugh.

He doesn't offer commentary or clever lines or explanations about men and machines and metaphors.

He just watches me finish the job.

Because even broken, bruised, and boiling with everything I still refuse to say aloud; this is mine.

The work, the ruin, the decision to keep going anyway.

It doesn't have to look pretty.

It just has to be finished.

And I'll be damned if I leave it half-done.

By the time the last crooked line of grass has been conquered, my arms ache and my jaw feels like it's been clenched for an hour straight. The mower finally relents with a sympathetic cough as I kill the engine and release the handle, the silence that follows somehow heavier than the machine's roar.

I survey the wreckage.

The yard is at least mowed, barely but the fence looks worse in the afternoon light. The panel is slumped halfway into the neighbor's yard, resting at an angle like it fainted mid-disagreement. Splinters dot the grass. One of the posts is cracked clean through, and the rosemary bush beneath it has suffered an indignity it may never recover from.

I wipe the back of my wrist across my forehead, then drop my hands to my hips, exhaling hard through the nose.

"Well," I mutter, "it's not like I was using my pride today."

Behind me, Benji finally shifts, stepping forward with the cautious energy of a man who's realized the lioness might not bite anymore, but still has teeth.

"You want help?" he offers, lifting his chin toward the wrecked panel. "I'm terrible at fences, but I'm excellent at pretending I know what I'm doing."

I glance at him. Then back at the fence.

And, for reasons I doesn't fully understand, I nod.

He jogs off toward the shed, humming something that might be a theme song or might just be nerves. By the time he returns, I already pulled the fallen panel out of the rosemary and leaned it upright against the remaining frame.

We work in near silence, if you can call it "working." It's more like shuffling pieces around with mounting confusion. The post is too far gone to brace properly, and every time we lift the panel, it droops on one side like it's mourning its own structural integrity. At one point, Benji tries to wedge it back in place with a brick and the handle of a rake.

"This is... going poorly," he admits, stepping back and squinting.

"You think?" I deadpan, holding the corner upright with my knee while trying to force a nail in at an impossible angle.

He doesn't reply right away, but when he does, his voice has lost its usual grin.

"Hey, listen. I'm gonna head out. I was just stopping by to check on JP anyway, and I think if I stay much longer, I'm gonna end up zip-tying this thing together and calling it 'modern rustic.'"

I let out a quiet breath. It's almost a laugh, almost a sigh at the same time and then I straighten.

"Thanks for... whatever that was."

Benji shrugs, adjusting his hoodie. "Hey. Everyone needs a witness sometimes."

He flashes one last grin much quieter now, almost real before turning toward the gravel path and heading to JP's, his footsteps fading against the gravel.

I stand there for a moment, fingers still curled around the edge of the crooked fence panel, my muscles tired, heart pounding for reasons that have nothing to do with lawn care.

And then I hear it.

The sound of tires rolling slowly over pavement. The crunch of gravel under wheels. The quiet groan of a truck door opening and closing.

I don't need to turn around.

I know exactly who it is.

Of course, he'd show up now; when my shirt is stuck to my back with sweat, there's dirt on my thighs and broken rosemary in my hair, when the fence is barely upright and my composure is holding together with emotional duct tape.

JP.

He doesn't call my name.

Doesn't announce himself.

Just approaches, footsteps even, the air around him cooling everything in a ten-foot radius like it always has.

I close my r eyes for half a second, just long enough to steady myself.

Then I turn.

I turn before he can speak, before he can pretend that showing up like this isn't exactly the kind of thing he does quietly, calculated, perfectly timed to make me feel like I'm the one who's overreacting.

"I'd say now's a bad time," I say, brushing my fingers against my temple where rosemary leaves cling like a crown of mockery, "but honestly, I'm not sure there's ever going to be a good one."

My voice is level, too level, the kind of steady that only comes when everything underneath is shaking. I don't meet his eyes right away. I don't have to. I know exactly what I'll see, their familiarity worn like armor, apology threaded into silence, and that frustrating way he always looks at me like I've already halfway forgiven him.

JP doesn't answer at first. He just stands there, a few feet away, hands tucked into his jacket pockets, watching me like he's afraid sudden movement might spook me. He looks the same taller than he should be, calm in the way still water can be calm right before it swallows you.

His gaze flicks to the leaning fence panel, then back to me.

"You've been busy," he says quietly.

I let out a short breath and half a laugh, half a warning. "Is that what we're going with?"

"I mean," he adds, eyes lingering on the crooked post, the half-repaired line, the scattered tools at her feet, "you've clearly made an impression."

The corners of my mouth twitch. Not a smile. Something colder.

"I wasn't trying to impress anyone," I say, still not looking directly at him. "I was just trying to get through my morning without everything falling apart."

JP nods, but the silence between us says more than the words. He shifts his weight slightly, the gravel beneath his boots crunching as he steps forward—not close enough to touch, but close enough that the air tightens.

"I didn't mean to drop in unannounced," he offers, soft, tentative, too late.

"Pretty sure you've made a habit of that," I murmur, turning my gaze toward him, now it's direct, clear, not biting yet, but dangerously close.

It lands.

He blinks. Just once.

And there it is.

The shift.

"I was coming to check on the house," he says. "I didn't know you'd be—"

"Still here?" I finish, voice clipped. "Messed up the timeline, did I?"

He opens his mouth, but no words come out. Not yet.

I exhale again, quieter this time, looking past him, over his shoulder, anywhere but straight into the heat of what's building between them.

And then, just barely above a whisper—

"It was just a fence."

But they both know it wasn't.

Not really.

JP doesn't respond right away. He just stands there, gaze flicking between the fallen fence panel, the half-dug post hole, and my dirt-smudged hands still curled around a rusted hammer like she's trying to remember why I bothered picking it up in the first place.

Then, quietly without a sigh, without a word he steps past me.

Not around. Not away.

Just... past.

To the fence.

He crouches low beside the sagging post, brushes some of the splintered earth away with one hand, and grips the loose panel with the other, testing its weight like he's checking for something familiar.

"I've got it," I say, sharper than I mean to, the words coming out brittle and fast.

"I know," he answers, still crouched, still not looking at me. "But it's easier with two hands."

I swallow. But I don't move.

JP rises, brushes off his palms, and heads toward the tools laid out in a crooked half-circle in the grass. He scans them, then selects a pair of work gloves and the claw hammer, checking its balance like its muscle memory. It probably is.

He returns to the panel, braces it with his knee, and doesn't wait for me to agree before he starts pulling the bent nails free.

I watch, with arms crossed, caught between the urge to kick him out of my disaster and the pull of something steadier, something less exhausting than keeping the wall up.

"You're not doing it right," I mutter, eyes narrowing at the way he wedges the board too high on one side.

His voice is quieter now, laced with something more honest. "It's not exactly a regulation fence."

I huff. "What does that even mean?"

"It means," he says, standing upright with one hand still on the board, "this whole thing's been patched so many times, it doesn't remember how it started."

I exhale slowly, the fight in my chest fading just enough to let the words settle.

There's no pity in his voice. No performative guilt. Just a shared acknowledgment of something broken being held together the best way two tired people know how.

I step toward him, slow and guarded, and pick up the second hammer.

"I'm not saying you're right," I mutter, lifting the board into place beside his hand, "but if this falls down again, I'm blaming you."

JP doesn't flinch.

"Deal."

We work in silence for a few minutes, each movement deliberate and wordless. Not smooth, not graceful, just steady. Nails go in. Boards creak. The scent of rosemary mixes with sun-warmed pine and the metallic tang of old tools.

At one point, our shoulders bump slightly as we lean in to align the next panel. Neither of them steps back.

It's not a truce. Not yet.

But it's something.

A start. A thread. A piece of wreckage they're willing, for now, to hold together.

By the time we finish, the fence is technically standing. It leans a little, the nails are crooked, and I'm pretty sure the rosemary bush will never forgive me but it's done, well sort of.

I drop the hammer into the grass and step back, pressing my hands to my lower back. Every muscle aches. I'm filthy, sweaty, and my pride's taken at least three direct hits.

JP stands beside me, wiping dirt off his hands like this is normal, like we do this all the time. Almost like we're not strangers with too much tension and a whole lot of silence between us.

He glances over. His mouth opens like he might say something.

I cut him off before he can get a single word out.

"You're not as scary as your eyebrows," I say, deadpan. "But you do try really hard."

He blinks only once. Then huffs out a laugh through his nose.

Not a real one no definitely not the kind that cracks anything open.

Just enough to prove he heard me.

I turn before he can recover and start toward the porch, peeling off my gloves as I go, heart still racing from everything and nothing all at once.

And that's when I see my phone buzzing on the step where I left it earlier. A new email, still open on the screen.

Subject line: Welcome to the Staff Team.

I swipe it open, barely registering the HR welcome fluff before my eyes lock on the name.

Head Coach: Jon Paul Callahan.

My stomach drops. My vision tunnels.

I read it again.

Coach Callahan.

JP.

Him.

Of course.

Of course.

I let out a breath I didn't know I was holding, stare out at the half-mangled yard, the fence we just pieced together with stubbornness and spite, and feel the coldest kind of clarity settle into my bones.

Tomorrow, I start work hopefully.

And I'll be doing it with *him*.

Chapter 4

JP

The conference room smells like new money and old problems. Fresh paint, white trim, and that just-installed carpet scent still fighting with the lemon polish on the table. Big enough to seat sixteen, but only half the chairs are filled with people who'd rather be in the rink than here.

It's 9:04 a.m. Too early for drama, but not too early for people to check their watches.

Coach Wilcox is at the head of the table, arms folded, not hiding the fact he'd rather skip this. A few department heads flip through glossy print packets labeled WILCOX WOLVES // BRAND REFRESH INITIATIVE like they're hoping the answer to the team's problems is hiding in the margins.

Me? I'm two seats from the end just close enough to speak if I have to, far enough to disappear if I don't.

The front chair is empty.

The door opens.

She's not rushing. Just... deliberate.

The execs step in first, and one of them clears his throat. "Alright, thanks for making time. This is Jenna Monroe she's going to be working with us on a trial basis."

Trial basis. There's the hook.

"Jenna has experience in marketing and rebranding back in the city," another exec adds, ignoring the skeptical looks from the coaches. "We can't agree on what direction this club should take, so we're letting her run a short-term project to see what sticks."

From the way Wilcox's jaw tightens, I'd bet good money he already has an opinion on how this is going to go.

Jenna sets her tablet down at the head of the table. Black blazer, hair pulled low, simple flats. She's not dressed like she's here to impress more like she's trying to keep the room from reading too much into her.

"Morning," she says, voice even. "This isn't about changing who the Wolves are just how people see us."

She clicks the remote, and the screen at the front of the room lights up with a sharper, sleeker wolf logo.

It takes about five seconds before the first jab lands. "That's nice," one of the assistant coaches says, leaning back in his chair. "But last I checked, logos don't win games."

"I'm aware," Jenna replies, keeping her tone neutral. She clicks to the next slide, but the projector lags, and the screen stutters in a way that makes a couple guys smirk.

Another coach, Daniels folds his arms. "We had a guy in here three years ago with the same pitch. Didn't work then either."

Jenna nods once, almost too quick, and I catch the faintest pause before she says, "Then let's figure out why."

It's not perfect. She's not commanding the room yet. But she doesn't retreat, either.

Benji, our assistant coach, leans in with a grin that means trouble. "Just don't put the wolf in a crop top and we're good."

Without missing a beat: "You sent me that idea in an email. I ignored it."

A few laughs fill the room, even Wilcox's mouth twitches.

"I'm just saying," Benji presses, "if we want to draw in a younger demographic—"

"Don't finish that sentence."

"I'm a visionary."

"You're a liability."

That gets a louder laugh. She glances up just long enough to catch his grin before flipping to the next slide.

She moves through brand pillars, community impact, social presence and the usual consultant menu, but I notice she's careful not to linger on anything too long. She's reading the room, trimming on the fly, steering around the harder glares from the coaches.

Then her gaze sweeps the table and lands on me." Head Coach Callahan. You've been quiet."

I sit back a little, not defensive, just measuring her. "I don't usually chime in until someone says something worth arguing with."

That gets another ripple of laughter.

"Fair," she says. "Then tell me then since you've been here longer than anyone in this room. What's missing?"

The room quiets, all that skepticism now focused squarely on me.

"What's missing," I say slowly, "is what happens on the ice. You can give the wolf a haircut and a marketing campaign, but it doesn't change the fact that the locker room feels like the season's over before it starts."

A few of the coaches nod faintly not in agreement so much as he's not wrong.

She doesn't flinch. Doesn't fire back. She just lets the words hang for a beat before saying, "Noted."

And she moves on.

The rest of the meeting is a tug-of-war. The coaches keep poking holes. She sidesteps where she can, answers where she has solid ground. I can tell she's not winning them over yet, but she's not losing either. For someone walking into a room full of people who'd rather be anywhere else, that's something.

By the time it's over, the execs are already moving her toward the hallway, probably to some upstairs meeting where the real decisions get made.

But just as she reaches the door, Daniels calls out, "Hey, Monroe. If your trial run doesn't work, you got a backup plan?"

She pauses for half a second, maybe less and then turns just enough to meet his eyes.

"Yeah," she says. "Not wasting my mornings in rooms where people already decided not to listen."

She doesn't wait for a response. Just walks out with the execs.

That earns her a couple of muttered comments from the table, but also one or two grudging smirks. Mine included.

A minute later, my phone buzzes.

JENNA: Your team thinks I'm funny.

I stare at it for a second before replying.

JP: You are. Annoyingly.

That's all I send. Because I'm still not sure if she's here to fix something...or just to see how far she can push before we push back

Chapter 5

Jenna

The cottage smells like vanilla, browned butter, and just a hint of frustration.

Sunlight pours through the open windows, spilling across the tile floors in long, golden strips. A breeze filters in from the lake, fluttering the edge of the checkered tea towel hanging from the oven handle. Somewhere outside, a bird sings like it's auditioning for a Disney movie. It's all very charming. Idyllic, even.

And I'm absolutely not enjoying any of it.

I've already cracked three eggs, two of which were supposed to go into the mixer but somehow ended up shell-shattered and emotionally symbolic in the sink.

The oven hums behind me at 350 degrees. My apron's smudged with flour. There's a tiny streak of chocolate on my cheek I haven't wiped off because I'm too busy replaying a stupid, two-line text conversation that shouldn't mean anything.

You are. Annoyingly.

It was supposed to be a throwaway line. A shrug of a message but somehow, it's looped itself into my brain like background music I can't shut off.

I dust cinnamon into the batter with a little more force than necessary.

The wooden spoon clatters against the bowl.

The room settles again; it's still, sunlit and quiet except for the low whirr of the ceiling fan and the distant buzz of bees in the hydrangeas outside. If peace were a place, this would be it.

So why am I pacing between the fridge and the counter like I'm waiting for a verdict?

Because I can't tell if JP Callahan was flirting... or just being himself.

And maybe that's the most dangerous part of all.

The cookies were supposed to be simple.

A peace offering to myself a little brown sugar therapy. A domestic flex in a borrowed kitchen that still doesn't know how to behave.

Instead, the second batch has started billowing smoke like I'm trying to signal for help in pastry code.

I fling open the oven door and a wave of burnt sugar and betrayal hits me square in the face. The smoke alarm screams overhead, a high-pitched banshee wail that only seems to mock me louder the more I panic.

"NO, NO, NO—" I shout, grabbing the nearest dish towel and flapping it at the ceiling like I'm trying to swat an airborne demon.

The fire extinguisher that I spotted behind the broom closet earlier and thought, how quaint. Now it's the last line of defense. I sprint for it, slam my hip into the counter, and hiss through my teeth. Smoke curls through the air like stage fog. The cookies are officially charcoal.

I rip the pin from the extinguisher, aim with the confidence of exactly zero training, and squeeze.

FWOOOSH.

A thick blast of white coats the inside of the oven, the stove, half the floor, and possibly my dignity.

That's when I hear the voice.

Low, unbothered and annoyingly amused.

"Is this part of your baking process, or should I be calling in backup?"

I whirl around.

Outside the open kitchen window with arms folded against the window frame like it's a bar counter stands JP Callahan.

Looking far too smug for someone who didn't just accidentally gas a tray of oatmeal chocolate chip with a fire extinguisher.

"Don't you have a team to yell at or a puck to tape?" I snap, waving residual smoke from my face.

He doesn't move.

"You always set off smoke alarms this early in the day?" he asks. "Or am I just lucky?"

I don't answer him.

Mostly because I'm still waving smoke and fire extinguisher dust out of my face and trying not to lose it over the tray of cookies that now look like they survived a house fire.

Then I hear it.

The front door.

Opening. Closing.

Boots on hardwood.

I freeze.

"You've got to be kidding me," I call, not bothering to turn around. "Is the whole town on some kind of 'just walk into Jenna's house' plan, or are you freelancing?"

No response. Just the sound of footsteps moving through the front room, slow and deliberate, like he's taking stock of the place.

And then there he is.

JP Callahan.

Leaning against the kitchen doorway, arms crossed like he's not totally sure how he ended up here but isn't planning to leave just yet.

His eyes take in the scene from the scorched baking tray, the blanket of white foam across the stove, the smoke alarm still flashing red in warning. Then me, standing in the middle of it all like a human disaster in an apron.

He doesn't say anything at first.

Then, quietly, like he's still working out if he's allowed to laugh: "You really went full fire extinguisher on cookies?"

I give him a look that could peel paint.

"They were on fire."

"They were smoking."

"Same thing."

He nods, like he's going to let me have that one even though he very much disagrees. Then he does the unthinkable like it's the most natural thing in the world, he pulls out one of the chairs at the table and sits down.

Like this is normal.

Like he does this all the time.

"You okay?" he asks, not looking at the mess this time—just me.

And it's not performative. He's not making fun. There's no smirk hiding in the corner of his mouth. Just... a question quiet and simple.

And real.

I swallow hard.

"I was just trying to bake," I say, setting the fire extinguisher down like it personally betrayed me. "It was supposed to be relaxing."

He leans back a little in the chair, eyes still on me.

"Therapy usually ends with less property damage."

That gets me.

I laugh before I can stop myself. It's short, surprised, from somewhere low in my chest. Not because it was that funny, but because something about the way he said it was exactly what I needed.

And suddenly, I don't feel quite so ridiculous.

Still covered in flour. Still standing in a kitchen that looks like a scene from a very niche horror movie. But… not alone.

I don't mean to say anything.

I really don't.

But there's something about him just sitting there, quiet, arms resting on his thighs like he's settled in for the long haul. He's not asking for more. Not even offering a solution. He's just there and present in that way that feels rarer than it should be.

So, the words sneak out sideways, like steam from a cracked lid.

"It wasn't supposed to be like this," I say, staring down at the streak of chocolate batter I smeared across the counter earlier and never cleaned up. "Any of it."

He doesn't speak.

I think that's what makes me keep going.

"I had this…life." I lift my hands, motion vaguely toward the ceiling, toward nothing. "A rhythm. The job, the city, the lease renewal reminder that made me feel like I was doing something right."

The laugh that escapes me is small and bitter.

"I even had a standing Wednesday night wine order and a dog I borrowed from my neighbor when I needed emotional support without commitment."

JP stays still, but something about his expression shifts just barely.

I glance over, testing his reaction and nothing. not even a smirk, no pity.

So, I keep going.

"Then the company tanked. Folded so fast, it felt like the walls got pulled off while we were still inside. We were in the middle of a product launch when they walked in with envelopes, like we were being voted off the island."

I press my fingers into the edge of the counter. It feels cool and solid grounding me.

"And I thought, okay, that's survivable. I've done hard things. I've watched YouTube tutorials on how to reframe your mindset."

JP huffs out a faint breath. I'm not sure if it's a laugh or just disbelief.

"But then," I say, and my voice drops a little, tightens at the edges, "I found out the guy I was dating had already filled the vacancy I left behind with someone younger, someone newly hired, someone with a better smile and a smaller dress size and apparently zero conflict about stealing my desk and my boyfriend."

That last part comes out sharper than I expect and I pause, not meaning to let that much out.

But it's too late to reel it back in.

JP's still watching me.

His elbows rest on his knees now, hands loosely clasped like he's sifting through what I just said—not judging it, not trying to fix it. Just holding it in place.

"She sounds like an idiot," he says quietly.

My laugh catches in my throat with a half laugh, half something else.

"Pretty sure it was a group effort, He made the idiot list, too."

"You deserve a better list."

I freeze.

His voice is low and rough in the kind of way that doesn't ask for attention, but keeps it anyway.

My hands drift to the back of my neck, fingers threading through the base of my hair. I'm suddenly aware of how ridiculous I must look with flour still on my cheek, kitchen a full-on crime scene, smoke alarm blinking behind me like it's still concerned.

"This place was supposed to be temporary," I say, softer now. "A landing pad, I needed to reset, to regroup. Not to fall apart in slow motion."

"And now?" he asks.

I lift my eyes to his.

Everything in me wants to dodge, to crack a joke or attempt to spin this into something lighter, But I don't.

"Now it feels like I'm standing in the ruins of what I thought my life was going to be. And trying to keep smiling like I didn't lose the blueprint in the fire."

JP nods, just once. Not with sympathy but with understanding. It's quiet, but heavy. A weight you only recognize if you've carried something similar.

There's silence.

But it's not uncomfortable.

It's the kind that fills the space between two people when nothing needs to be said but everything's been heard.

Then he leans back, stretching slightly, eyes drifting around the kitchen.

"You ever think about what comes after the blueprint burns?" he asks.

I raise an eyebrow.

"You rebuild."

He shrugs. "Maybe, or maybe you design something better."

I blink, unsure whether that's the most profound or most dangerously hopeful thing I've heard in months.

Maybe both.

Before I can respond, the smoke alarm lets out one last dying beep and then goes silent like even it knows the moment's passed.

JP stands slowly, brushing his hands against his jeans.

"I'll let you get back to... fireproofing your cookies," he says, the barest hint of dry humor in his voice.

I smile, small and sideways.

"Thanks for the uninvited visit and unexpected therapy."

He pauses near the door.

Then glances back at me with something in his eyes I haven't seen before.

"Next time, just text. Less risk of smoke inhalation."

And then he's gone.

Just like that.

But he leaves something behind in the air.

Stillness.

And the faintest scent of hope under all the smoke.

After the door clicks shut behind him, the silence settles in again. But it feels different this time, not heavy and definitely not hollow just still.

I glance around the kitchen. There's flour on the floor, a smudge of chocolate on the fridge, and foam dust clinging to everything like snow that forgot how to melt.

And on the far corner of the baking tray a miracle of miracles, one cookie survived.

Mostly.

The edges are dark, but the center looks soft, chewy and warm.

Kind of like me, maybe.

I peel it off the tray with a spatula and sink onto the bench by the window, tucking one leg beneath me. The cushion is lumpy. The breeze still smells faintly like burnt sugar.

Outside, JP's walking across the yard. Hands in his pockets, head down, like he's turning something over in his mind. He doesn't look back.

Not once.

But I watch him anyway.

And take a bite of the cookie.

Still warm.

Still sweet.

Still here.

Chapter 6

JP

The truck engine clicks as it cools, one faint tick after another, like it's counting down to something I haven't named yet.

I sit for a few seconds after I cut it off.

Window cracked just enough to let in the crisp edge of early morning. The kind of air that tastes like cold metal and feels like home. Not the cozy, fireside kind no this kind of home is colder, harder. Earned. Like you have to keep showing up for it.

The suns just started to rise over the ridge, casting the whole parking lot in a pale, gold-gray wash. Long shadows stretch from the arena walls like arms reaching backward into memory. The pavement's still damp from the night dew, but dry enough that my boots will crunch when I hit the gravel.

I let the silence stretch.

The arena looms ahead, solid and plain, its cinderblock face stained by time and weather. No frills, no distractions, just walls. The kind that doesn't ask questions they just hold everything in.

I breathe in and then out.

The kind of breath that settles deeper than lungs. The kind that lives in your ribs and in the backs of your shoulders, where years of pressure never quite loosen.

I pop the door open.

The sound of my boots hitting the lot is sharp. Clean. The arena's back door is about thirty paces from my truck around thirty slow steps through the quiet before the rest of the day starts breathing down my neck.

Each step echoes a little.

Wilcox's Jeep is already here, parked crooked, nothing new there. Two maintenance vans near the loading dock, and a dented Civic I recognize from one of the rink techs and that's it. No players yet and no noise. Just the slow inhale of the building as it wakes up.

I walk with my hands in my jacket pockets. The wind picks up just enough to tug at the edge of my collar.

The closer I get, the more it seeps in the scent of cold steel and scraped ice. A chill beneath the concrete is familiar like walking into a place that remembers you even when you don't want to be remembered.

I pause at the threshold.

This place has held every version of me from rookie, enforcer, captain and now coach. It's seen me bruised, bleeding, celebrated, cussed out, and everything in between.

Some days, it feels like a sanctuary.

Other days, like a cage.

Today? I'm not sure yet.

I push open the door and step into the tunnel.

Lights hum overhead. The hallway stretches long and empty, with posters peeling slightly at the corners and a faint clatter from somewhere deeper inside—probably the skate sharpener warming up.

My steps echo.

The door gave way with a familiar groan as I stepped inside, the sound echoing across the empty locker room like a voice calling back through time. The place was still like the kind of stillness that settles after the storm of bodies and noise has long cleared, leaving only the bones of a ritual behind. No voices, no scent of fresh tape or the laughter that usually bled out of these walls after a good scrimmage. Just the residual hush of a room that used to mean more.

I moved slowly, my boots landing solid against the concrete, each step measured as though my feet remembered the rhythm even if my mind didn't. The benches were already scuffed from the early shift bags slouched against stalls, a water bottle half-full and forgotten on the floor. Everything looked touched but not occupied, as if the boys had come and gone, or were on the ice already, their energy leaving behind only traces of presence.

I paused in the center of the room, hands still in the pockets of my jacket, and let the silence wrap around me. It wasn't empty, not really. The silence here had weight with memories. It carried echoes of all the noise that used to live in this space and booming voices, sharp jokes, the low rumble of pre-game focus, and the post-win chaos that smelled like sweat, beer, and something just shy of joy.

And for a moment, without warning or effort, I was back in it.

I saw it clearly, my younger self tossing gloves into an open bag with one hand while chirping the rookie about a missed pass. Wilcox laughing so hard he had to lean against the stall, someone blasting a playlist that made no sense, and nobody caring because the vibe was right. That kind of atmosphere you didn't have to earn with words it just existed when the team was right. It was kinetic, electric and back then, I didn't second-guess my place in it.

Back then, my name still carried weight as a player.

Not just a coach.

Not just a man in the corner taking notes and counting ice time.

But that version of me had been peeled away like old tape after an injury. Stripped back until all that remained was the quieter version, the one who had learned how to carry things in silence. How to rebuild with his mouth closed and his fists unclenched.

I lowered myself to the edge of the bench, leaning forward with elbows braced against my knees. The wood creaked beneath me, familiar and solid. I sat there for a long moment, staring at nothing in particular, just the rows of lockers, the empty hooks, the worn padding, the ghost of something I couldn't name.

This room didn't need me to speak.

It never had.

But sometimes, I wished it remembered me the way I remembered it.

I exhaled slowly, pressing the breath out through my nose, jaw locked tight. I could've stayed here another five minutes, easy probably another ten. Let the ghosts talk to me while the cold sunk deeper into the concrete and the overhead lights kept humming like they knew better than I did how the day would go.

But there's a limit to nostalgia. You can feel it edge in just enough to remind you who you were but if you let it settle too long, it'll convince you that version of you was better. Untouchable.

And I don't have time for that kind of lie.

"Alright," I muttered, voice low, rough in the empty space. "That's enough."

I stood, slow but steady, letting my body stretch the way it always does after too many hours bent under the weight of memory and not enough sleep. My knees cracked, nothing new. The stiffness wasn't from age, not entirely. It was just the cost of having been too much for too long.

My gear bag sat by the stall like it had been waiting, zipper half-undone from the last time I forgot to repack it right. I kicked it open and crouched down, fingers already sorting through pads and skates on instinct. The act itself was comforting, like ritualistic in a way few things are anymore.

Jersey, pads, socks and the tape roll that's always almost out.

I dressed in silence, the way I used to when a game meant everything, but the pressure hadn't yet bled into my bones. Every strap, every loop, every pull of laces brought me back to a center I didn't realize I'd left.

Helmet last, always last.

The visor slightly smudged, the chin strap frayed, but still mine.

I picked it up, gave it one last look, and settled on it like a soldier pulling on a battered helmet. It's less for protection now and more for principle.

No speeches, no fire-up playlist.

Just a man putting himself back together one piece at a time.

And then I opened the locker room door and stepped into the corridor that led straight to the ice.

Because ready or not this is who I am.

And some mornings, that's enough.

The walk from the tunnel to the edge of the ice felt like crossing into another life; one stitched together from muscle memory, silence, and the echo of every time I'd laced up with something to prove.   I could hear the team laughing and buzzing through the walls as it echoed, and the odd parents who stayed to watch their children practice. It was time for me to head out to the ice and coach my team. The boards curved ahead, the plexiglass reflecting light in that distorted, watery way it always had, and for a moment, the air seemed to still entirely, thick with the kind of anticipation that didn't belong to games anymore, but to legacies.

As I reached the opening, the speaker system above crackled to life with a brief whine, drawing the heads of every player still coasting lazily across the rink, and then the voice came—confident, level, just loud enough to cut through the chill in the air.

"Ladies and gentlemen... please welcome back to the ice... former captain of the Titans, Head Coach... Jon Paul Callahan."

No dramatic music followed, no video montage, just the name, my full name. Spoken with the same formality they used when they retired numbers, or raised banners, or announced legends stepping into the building for the last time. But this wasn't a farewell. Not yet.

Skates stilled, pucks stopped moving and laughter cut off mid-sentence as every face on the ice, whether veteran or rookie, turned toward the tunnel where I stood, gloves still gripped tightly in the other, chest already rising and falling with the steady pace of focus honed over years of knowing how to command a room without ever needing to say a word.

I stepped forward onto the ice.

The first glide was instinctual, my blade catching the surface with a satisfying hiss, balance held low and centered, shoulders squared. The air was colder out here, sharper somehow, like the ice recognized me and had been waiting. I didn't look up to meet their eyes. I didn't raise a hand or smile or nod. I just moved, cutting a long, clean arc through the neutral zone, the kind of path you make when you're not here to prove you belong, but to remind everyone you never *stopped*.

I skated once around center, not fast, but smooth and direct, letting the silence around me stretch until it held something close to reverence. Wilcox stood at the far end, arms crossed, grinning with unspoken commentary. A couple of the younger players exchanged wide-eyed glances, the sort of look that lives somewhere between awe and disbelief. One mouthed something to his teammate and caught himself just in time, the kind of near-swear that gets overlooked when a ghost walks back into your locker room and starts carving lines into the ice again.

I stopped near the bench, turned back toward the center, and planted both blades with purpose—still not saying a word.

Because nothing needed to be said.

Sometimes, it's not the volume of a return that makes people pay attention.

It's the silence you carry when you do.

The weight of the silence didn't press down on me; it held the space open, cleared it, like a rink before first skate. No one moved, sticks hung loose in gloves and players hovered just outside of formation. They were unsure whether to break into drills or keep watching, like they weren't sure if this was a return or a reckoning.

I turned to face them, and only then did I remove my helmet, sliding it off slowly and letting the air touch my sweat-damp hair. I held it under my arm, shoulders square, eyes sweeping the lineup not dramatically, not in some commanding gesture, but with quiet calculation. I was seeing them, and they were seeing me, and that was enough to make the moment feel like something more than routine.

"You all know who I am," I said, voice low but carried across the rink with clarity. "You've seen the jersey hanging on the wall, or heard the stories from guys like Wilcox, or maybe just Googled the name when you got here. Doesn't matter."

I paused, let the words settle.

"What matters is this; I'm not out here to prove anything. Not to you. Not to myself. I've already done that, years ago. What I'm here for now is to build something that lasts longer than any one name on the back of a sweater."

A few players shifted their weight, the kind of adjustment you make when you're not used to someone talking like this, not yelling, not cracking jokes. Just telling the truth in a voice that doesn't shake.

"We've got a season coming. A rebrand. New leadership. New expectations. Maybe some of you are worried about that and how good you should be. Change means pressure, and pressure separates contenders from background noise."

Another pause, this one weighing heavier.

"I'm not interested in background noise."

I let my eyes linger on the youngest player, he's barely out of juniors, still with that wide, eager stance like he hadn't learned how to carry doubt yet.

"If you're not skating like every shift counts, if you're not show-ing up like it's the job that pays your rent and feeds your family, if you're not listening and I mean really listening to the people who've already been through it and come out scarred on the other side... then you won't last."

Wilcox gave a soft whistle behind me. It wasn't sarcastic this time. Just approval, quiet and sharp.

"But if you're ready to bleed for this team, to sweat, to break and rebuild, to get comfortable with being uncomfortable... then we've got a shot at something real."

I stepped forward, not toward any one player, but toward the space between them. The center.

"I'm not your buddy and I'm certainly not your babysitter, I'm your coach. I'll fight for every one of you who fights back. But I won't carry dead weight."

That landed.

They weren't looking at a man making a comeback anymore.

They were looking at their coach.

And in that frozen moment between past and present, between silence and motion they knew exactly what that meant.

The team slowly returned to motion, scattering back into drills with a little more sharpness in their strides, like they'd felt the shift in the air and were trying to skate it off. Wilcox nodded to me once before blowing his whistle, sending them into rotation. My role, for now, was complete.

But I didn't move.

Not right away.

Because just past the bench, near the auxiliary tunnel by the zamboni bay, a small figure stood with her hands pressed to the plexiglass, her face tilted up in that wide-eyed way only seven-year-olds can manage without losing their balance or their dignity.

She was bundled in a too-big hoodie that nearly swallowed her arms, the sleeves pulled over her hands and her boots were untied. A notebook, or maybe a sketchpad, was tucked beneath one arm like it was her most precious belonging.

Maisie Hartley.

It took half a second for the recognition to hit. The hair, the mouth with both her parents staring back at me in miniature, even though one of them hadn't been around in a long time, and the other had been gone entirely for longer than she should've.

I didn't know she'd be here today though I hadn't asked. Maybe part of me had avoided knowing.

She didn't wave, didn't smile, she just looked at me, studied me. Like I was a riddle she halfway understood.

And for a flicker of a moment, I forgot about rebrands and broken careers and the stubborn hollow in my chest that coaching only sometimes filled. I forgot about standing on ice that had once been a battlefield. Forgot that I wasn't supposed to care this much anymore.

Because in her eyes, I wasn't the fallen player, or the silent coach, or the man who spent more time inside his own head than outside the rink.

In her eyes—I was still someone.

Still his teammate.

Still her Coach Callahan.

I gave a slight nod, subtle and slow. Nothing performative. Just... acknowledgement. Connection. She mirrored it instantly, then tilted her head and mouthed something I couldn't hear.

I stepped closer to the glass.

"What was that?" I asked, half to myself, half hoping the sound might travel.

Maisie leaned in. No hesitation. Just certainty.

"You skate differently when you think no one's watching."

My chest tightened, a sharp pull I hadn't expected. Not pain. Not exactly. Just the kind of truth only a kid can drop without realizing they're cutting you wide open.

Before I could respond, she turned and skipped off her hood bouncing, boots still untied, vanishing through the back gate and into the echo of footsteps in the hall.

And just like that, the silence in my ribs shifted.

It didn't disappear.

But it made room for something else.

Something I hadn't carried in a long time.

Purpose.

Chapter 7

Jenna

The porch swing squeaks in a rhythm I've stopped noticing, a background soundtrack to the mid-afternoon lull that settles like a weight across my thighs. The cookies after round two; this time less charred, more edible and cooling beside me on a wire rack that wobbles every time I shift my leg. I'm not proud of how long I've been sitting here, half-hiding behind a hanging fern and pretending I'm deeply invested in neighborhood bird patterns.

But when JP's truck rumbles down the street and pulls into the drive across from mine, I stop pretending.

He gets out slow. Not tired, exactly more like his body's still unwinding from something intense. His hair's damp at the edges, curling a little where his helmet must've pressed. He's got his duffel slung over one shoulder and a gait that's too smooth to be accidental. This isn't a man dragging himself home, this is someone who knows how to carry weight, literal or not.

He doesn't head inside right away.

Instead, he pauses on the steps, one boot on the riser, and presses the heel of his palm to his sternum like he's checking that everything's still intact beneath the armor. It's a small thing and maybe he doesn't know he's doing it. Or maybe he does, and just doesn't care that someone might be watching.

Because I am watching.

Not spying, no not really but... observing with interest.

There's something raw about him right now. He's not vulnerable, not in the way people use that word when they mean soft. No this is a man who's quietly unraveling, just a little, behind the privacy of a porch and a locked jaw. His shoulders drop as he breathes out, slow and long, like whatever he faced today scraped more off the surface than he expected.

He drops the bag by the door and leans on the railing with both hands, staring out across the space between us. Not at me. Just... out. Like he's trying to find something in the air he can't quite name.

And I sit there, in my flour-dusted shorts with a half-burnt cookie in hand, watching a man I've mentally labeled as brooding, difficult, and emotionally constipated slowly unfold like a story someone forgot to finish reading.

The strangest part?

I don't hate it.

As the day goes on, I find myself exploring a trail that winds out past the last of the cottages; it doesn't have a name, and I'm not entirely sure it's even meant to be a trail. But the ground is worn from enough foot traffic to suggest I'm not the first woman who needed to walk something off in the middle of the afternoon. I didn't plan the route and I barely planned the shoes but my body wanted motion, and my brain well, it needed space. Space to stretch and unravel and maybe stitch itself back together along the way.

I pass under a canopy of tangled limbs, brittle leaves whispering secrets overhead, and I let my fingertips skim over the long grasses and sun-bleached fence posts that haven't seen fresh paint in years. Everything out here feels a little forgotten, like the world stepped away for a moment and left it breathing on its own. It's comforting in a way I didn't expect. Still, but not hollow. Solitary, but not lonely.

The closer I get to the lake, the quieter things become. Not in a dramatic, cinematic kind of way but in the bone-deep hush of a place that has held grief before and kept going anyway. I breathe a little deeper, my heartbeat finding a rhythm that isn't tangled in deadlines or people's expectations or the weight of trying to outrun failure.

When the lake finally appears through the trees it's flat and steel-colored, with light slicing across its surface like a blade that stops me. Not because it's beautiful, though it is, in a raw, un-Instagrammable kind of way. But because it's still. So still, it feels like I've stepped out of my life entirely, like I've slipped into a pocket of time that doesn't require me to be anything but here.

I make my way to the dock and lower myself down to sit near the edge, legs dangling just above the water, sneakers hovering over their own warped reflection. I don't cross my arms or curl up tight. I just sit there, open and quiet, like maybe the lake can read minds and it'll answer back if I stay long enough.

For a while, I let my thoughts wander into soft, shapeless things I don't usually let out in daylight. About how hard it is to rebuild when people only ever see the wreckage. About how I hate that I still flinch when I hear my ex's name, or how part of me wonders if I'll ever be truly good at anything again. Not just okay, but *undeniably good*.

I think about what it means to start over at thirty when the version of your life you were supposed to be living was already monogrammed and mapped and halfway planned in a Pinterest board you never had the nerve to delete.

And then, just when the quiet starts to settle into something like peace, I hear it.

The crunch of gravel behind me.

Footsteps that are steady and rhythmic. Close enough that I don't have to turn around to know it's someone who runs often and knows how to land soft.

I twist just enough to glance back over my shoulder, and there he is.

JP.

Jogging shirt damp with sweat, clinging in all the inconvenient places, shoulders broad and tense like the run hadn't quite worked whatever he was trying to outrun. He slows the moment he sees me his stride faltering, not dramatically, just enough to register surprise or maybe hesitation. He could turn around but he doesn't.

He stops just short of the dock, hands on his hips, eyes scanning the lake like he hadn't expected anyone else to claim the silence today.

"Didn't know this trail came out here," I say, because it's either that or Wow, you look like an entire problem and I'm trying not to stare.

He lifts a shoulder, still catching his breath. "It's usually empty."

I look back toward the water, letting the tension settle, but it doesn't rush to fill the space like I expected it to. Instead, something softer arrives, something quieter.

He steps onto the dock slowly, shoes clicking against the worn wood, and lowers himself down beside me not close enough to crowd, but not leaving much room for distance either. We sit like that for a moment, the dock creaking beneath our weight, the breeze tugging at the edges of my sweatshirt.

"I used to come out here after games," he says eventually. His voice is rougher than usual, not defensive, just honest. "Sometimes after wins. Mostly after losses."

I nod, letting the weight of that confession settle between us.

"Why'd you stop?"

He's quiet for a second too long "Felt like I didn't belong anymore."

The simplicity of it makes my chest tighten.

Not because it's dramatic. Because it's *true*.

And suddenly, we're not just sitting by a lake.

We're sitting in the middle of a question neither of us knows how to ask: where do you go when the thing that defined you forgets your name? kind of question.

Neither of us says it aloud.

But I think, just for a moment, he hears it in me too.

The quiet stretches between us, but it doesn't feel hollow. It feels more like a thread pulled tight, delicate and invisible, binding us to this moment and daring either of us to move first.

I don't know what JP's thinking. But I know how his presence feels.

Grounded, solid and a little dangerous in the way gravity is where you don't notice how much you're leaning into it until you're already falling.

He turns toward me, slow and deliberate, and the look in his eyes makes the air between us collapse. It's not cautious. It's not curious. It's *clear*.

Like he's made a decision. Or maybe given up resisting one.

I feel it before I see it the slight shift in his posture, the tension in his shoulders softening just enough for something else to rise. His gaze flickers to my mouth, then back to my eyes. His breath catches and while mine stumbles.

Then he leans in.

Every part of me goes still, like my body has finally caught up to the storm in my chest. There's no witty comment on my tongue. No fast-talking shield. Just the crackling knowledge that something is about to change.

His hand hovers at the edge of my jaw, not quite touching, but so close I can feel the warmth of it.

And I want him to do it.

God, I want him to do it.

To close the distance. To let this tension break into something we both stop pretending we don't feel.

But just before his lips reach mine—

he pulls back.

Fast and abrupt. Like he suddenly remembered who we are, and what this isn't allowed to be.

His eyes shutter.

He exhales hard, stepping away like space might help him get control again, but he looks anything but in control. His hands go to his hips. His jaw locks. And the warmth that was there a moment ago disappears, sealed behind the same wall I've been staring at since the day we met.

I blink, still caught in the aftershock. "Why did you stop?"

He swallows, but doesn't look at me. "Because if I didn't..." He trails off, shaking his head.

"Then what?"

He finally meets my eyes again.

And it's all there the truth, raw and unguarded.

"Then I wouldn't be able to stop."

The words hit like a confession and not dramatic just real.

And I don't know what to say to that. Because he's not saying he doesn't want me. He's saying he does; too much.

He takes a step back, like that inch of space will protect us both but I don't follow.

I sit there, still, heart pounding, skin flushed with the weight of almost.

And as he turns to leave, he's quiet, controlled, like he didn't just unravel everything and I watch him walk away, knowing one thing with absolute, breath-stealing certainty:

That kiss didn't happen. It just hasn't happened *yet*.

Chapter 8

JP

The arena exhales around me, a slow, familiar breath steeped in ice and memory. Every steel beam and scuffed board hums with ghosts, the scrape of blades from games long finished, the thunder of a crowd that once chanted my name. The cold clings to the air like a second skin, curling into my lungs with each inhale, sharp and sobering. That scent is sharpened steel, rubber, old sweat baked into the benches—wraps around me like an old jersey, worn thin with time and meaning.

I stand at the edge of the rink, arms folded tight across my chest, as if I can hold the past in place with sheer will. The boards groan faintly beneath my weight. I've learned here before many years ago, when my only worry was getting drafted, not staying whole. The lights overhead buzz with low electricity, casting long shadows across the ice, and for a second, I see us. The old team that's younger, lighter and untouched by grief.

The first pair of kids burst through the tunnel, skates slung over their shoulders, their voices echoing off the empty seats like birds startled into flight. They're loud and clumsy but alive in a way I'm not sure I remember how to be. One kid's helmet slips from under his arm and skitters across the rubber mats. He chases after it with a grin too big for his face, yelling something I don't catch but the joy in it punches straight through me.

They settle in by the benches, kneeling to tie their laces with fingers too eager, too fast. It's chaos, loose and imperfect, but it's sacred all the same. I've seen this moment play out a hundred times with boys becoming players, learning the weight of the game before they even know the rules of the world.

And still, every time, it knocks something loose inside me. Something I buried deep the day I hung up the pro jersey and swore I'd never come back. But this place... it remembers. And standing here now, I'm not sure if it's haunting me or calling me home.

I blow the whistle once it's short, sharp. It cracks through the noise and bounces off the rafters like it always has. The kids scramble into a loose formation at center ice, helmets crooked, jerseys flapping over elbow pads, like little warriors trying on armor two sizes too big. Some skate with confidence while others wobble like fawns. All of them look up at me like I hold the secret to something bigger than just hockey.

I don't. Not anymore.

But I nod like I do like this is second nature, like I'm not aching under the weight of memory with every drill I call out. "Line up. Let's warm up the legs. Down and back. Go."

Blades hiss across the ice in staggered rhythm, a symphony of effort and inexperience. One kid forgets to stop at the boards and crashes, sprawling like a starfish. The others laugh, not cruel but the kind of joy that comes easy when life hasn't bruised you yet. I smile before I can stop myself.

I skate backward, watching and coaching. Correcting a stance here, a stick angle there. The words come without thinking. "Knees bent, Isaac. You're not a folding chair." He adjusts mid-glide, grinning at the joke, and I see a spark of something I used to chase; a need to get it right, to be better, to belong.

Ten minutes in, the rhythm takes hold. They're sweating. Focused. And I forget, for a moment, that I ever left this ice behind. That the arena never went quiet for me.

Then one of them, Hudson, the smallest skates over, brow furrowed in frustration, one skate lagging like it's fighting him. "Coach, it keeps coming loose."

He's trying not to let it bother him, but I see the sting in his eyes. The way he wants so badly to keep up.

"Let me see," I say, crouching beside him.

The laces are uneven and one pull away from tripping him mid-drill. I take the boot, fingers moving from muscle memory, looping and tugging like I did for Maisie's dad during travel league back in juniors.

Hudson watches, quiet now, eyes wide.

"There," I murmur, tightening the final knot with a sharp tug. "Won't come undone unless you're flying."

He beams, not at the skate but at me like I just gave him permission to believe in himself.

And for the first time in longer than I care to admit, I wonder if maybe this is what it's all about, not the roar of pro arenas, not the endless road games or high-stakes playoff tension maybe this is what the game was always supposed to be about.

I'm still crouched beside Hudson when the squeak of the side door echoes through the rink. I don't have to look to know who it is when the sound is followed by the telltale rhythm of boots scuffing rubber mats like they own the damn place.

"Look at you," Benji calls out, voice carrying like a puck off the glass. "Big softie with a half hitch knot. Never thought I'd see the day."

I rise slowly, letting the smirk settle before I face him. "You're late."

"Fashionably," he grins, strolling toward the boards with a coffee in one hand and trouble in the other. His Sea Dogs hoodie is half-zipped, revealing a T-shirt that reads Puck Off, and his hair's got that slept-in-my-truck charm he somehow gets away with.

Hudson skates off to rejoin the others. Benji leans on the boards beside me, watching the drills like he might actually care even though we both know he came for a different reason.

"You're good with them," he says casually. "Better than you let on."

I grunt, keeping my eyes on the kids.

A beat and then "So. How's your city girl?"

I turn my head just enough to give him a look that's flat and warning.

Benji just grins wider, sipping his coffee like it's spiked with mischief. "The one with the good hair and the don't-talk-to-me face. I saw her yesterday near the bakery. It looked like she was trying to disappear into her scarf."

"She's none of your business."

"Didn't say she was. Just noticed you've been moodier than usual lately, and you only get that way when a woman's involved or when the Leaf's win. But mostly women."

I shake my head, but he keeps going, relentlessly.

"Come on, JP are you skating drills or dodging feelings today? Because either way, it's starting to show." He pauses dramatically. "Even Maisie asked me if you were in love."

That lands like a puck to the ribs.

"How does Maisie know Jenna?" I ask curiosity getting the better of me."

Benji gives me a look, "You do realize Jenna is helping rebrand the association, and Maisie is usually around in the rink, right? They were bound to run into each other and the looks you two give each other when no one is watching...Even a kid can catch onto"

This woman is intertwining with my life without me even knowing it.

I just give Benji a shrug trying to play it off like that's not actually true but it makes me second guess even my own thoughts. By the time I go to say something Bengi is already replying to himself.

Benji chuckles, eyes dancing. "Swear to God. 'Are you in love with Miss Jenna yet?' Like it's a kindergarten dare. Kid's have instincts."

I don't answer because I still don't have one.

Instead, I blow the whistle, louder this time. The boys snap to attention.

"Back to work!" I bark, skating toward center ice.

But as I move, I feel Benji's eyes still on me, amused and curious.

And beneath all that noise, one truth slinks in cold and quiet, I hate that he's not wrong.

The final whistle slices clean through the rink's hum, a sharp punctuation that sets the kids loose in a burst of chaotic energy. Gear clatters, voices rise, and their laughter echoes off the rafters like music from another life. Practice ends as it always does—on a note of joy too loud to ignore and too far from the silence I carry with me.

I stay behind, slow in the way I move, gathering pucks across the ice while the world around me winds down. Benji handles the stragglers, his voice easy, his presence loud enough to cover whatever mine lacks. He's good at that, at filling space, drawing attention away from the things I'd rather not explain.

"See you next week, Coach!" one of the boys calls out, cracking voice wrapped in pride and sweat.

I lift a hand in reply, but I'm already gone.

Not physically. Not yet.

But my mind has left the rink, pulled by something quieter, steadier. With old cedar boards and a bent railing. A house I shouldn't look for, but do anyway. A woman I shouldn't care about, but do more than I'll ever say out loud.

She's not mine, not really but there are moments though small, fleeting things that make me wonder if she feels it too. The way her eyes hold mine for a second too long or how we've started sharing details of our past traumas together. We never talk about it, maybe we are both afraid too or just waiting for the other to say something first. I should have kissed her by the lake and maybe I ruined it.

The last of the kids cleared out ten minutes ago. Their laughter still echoes faintly off the boards, but the rink's gone completely still now, just the hum of the lights. I reach for my clipboard, gloves tucked under one arm and I make myself walk.

The cold hits harder once I step outside, slicing through the warmth I'd built up on the ice. The sky has shifted into something sullen; it's low and gray, the kind that carries snow in its gut but refuses to let it fall. Streetlamps hum to life one by one, soft halos blinking through the dusk as the town exhales into quiet.

I should head home. There's leftover soup in the fridge, a flannel blanket that still smells faintly of campfire, a pile of mail I keep meaning to sort. There are plenty of reasons to go the other way.

But none of them are strong enough.

I cut down the back alley instead, my boots crunching through patches of old salt, shoulders hunched against the wind. I don't rush, I let the quiet settle over me, let the dark press in. Let the questions stir.

Halfway down the block, I hear the scrape of a door and the jingle of the old brass bell from the back of the bakery. Miss Edie stands in the doorway in her flour-dusted apron, arms folded, hip cocked like she's been waiting for me.

"Was wondering how long it'd take you to come this way," she says, not quite smiling.

I stop mid-step. "Are you waiting for me, or just guarding the cinnamon rolls?"

She snorts softly and ducks back inside. When she returns, she's holding a small paper bag, steam rising faintly from the fold at the top. She presses it into my hand without ceremony.

"For the girl," she says.

I glance down at the bag, then back at her. "She didn't order anything."

"No," Edie says, meeting my eyes. "But she's been looking like she needs something warm. You've been looking like you want to be the one to give it to her."

I don't say anything.

She waves me off like she doesn't need me to. "Even quiet men need a spark, JP. You know that."

Her words land somewhere deep. Somewhere old.

I nod once. A quiet thank you.

And keep walking.

The houses blur past in soft outlines with strings of white lights blinking against porch rails, windows glowing gold from inside. It's the kind of night made for stories and secrets. For choosing to turn toward something, instead of away.

The bag in my hand radiates heat with a single cinnamon roll that's still warm. Wrapped in kindness and a little bit of mischief. Miss Edie doesn't meddle often, but when she does, it matters.

I take the long way to her street. Past the bookstore with its hand-painted sign that's started to peel. Thoughts of meeting Jenna for the first time crosses my mind her wrestling with her over packed suitcase with all her belongings tumbling out in every direction. It's the way she looked up at him, half annoyed, half embarrassed and had stuck with him ever since. These thoughts of her had invaded every point of his life to the point everyone else could see our chemistry even if I couldn't admit it to myself. Past the silence in me that's grown too comfortable.

When her house comes into view, I slow.

The porch is exactly how I left it. Slumped to one side. One corner post-split clean through at the base, as if the wood gave up on being strong a long time ago. I know that feeling.

The light in her window glows soft. One lamp with no movement behind it. The kind of quiet that either means she's not home or that she is, but she's trying not to be seen.

She didn't ask me to come.

She didn't ask me to care.

But I'm standing here anyway. Cold hands, aching heart, cinnamon roll in a paper bag like it means something.

Because tonight, I need to fix something that isn't me.

And maybe this porch is the only place I know how to start.

The porch groans beneath my step as I climb up, careful not to put weight on the side that's already sagging. I set the paper bag down on the top stair, the cinnamon roll inside still giving off a faint trace of warmth, like it's holding onto the memory of a fire long gone out.

The boards creak as I shift, crouching low to examine the damage. Up close, it's worse than I remembered. It's splintered through in two places, one post nearly hollow at the base, rotted from years of being ignored. The rail's loose too, the kind of loose that makes you think it's safe until it suddenly isn't.

I don't knock. Don't announce myself.

Just reach into the tool bag and get to work.

The first nail squeals as I pry it loose with metal on metal, loud in the stillness. I wince and I try to be gentler with the next one, but there's no way to do this quietly. The claw of the hammer slips, scraping the side rail with a sharp grind.

Another nail, another loud creak the wood shifts with a tired sigh as I remove the worst of the slats, stacking them off to the side like broken promises. Thinking to myself this is my sister's cabin and I never once thought I should fix it up while she's been gone, but with Jenna here I can't help myself I need to be around her even if it's just showing up unannounced or fixing things up, I know she can't do on her own. I'm focused, maybe too focused so when the screen door behind me creaks open, it catches me off guard.

"You always break into people's porches like this?"

Her voice slices through the night; it's dry and flat. Edged with confusion and something warmer buried underneath.

I pause with one knee on the step; hand still wrapped around the hammer.

Then I look up.

She's leaning against the doorway in a worn cardigan and leggings; hair piled messily on her head like she gave up fighting with it hours ago. There's a faint smudge of something near her temple, maybe flour, maybe paint, maybe proof she's been trying to stay busy in the way people do when they're trying not to feel something too loud.

The porch light hits her just right. Soft, gold, unfair.

I clear my throat. "You had a safety hazard."

"So, you just... showed up with tools?"

"I came from the rink." I gesture toward the street. "Had them in the truck."

"And the cinnamon roll?" she nods toward the bag I forgot was there.

"That's from Miss Edie," I say. "She told me to give it to you."

Jenna raises a brow. "Did she now."

"Said you looked like someone who needed something warm."

Her expression shifts, just barely. A flicker of something between surprise and heartbreak before she catches it, wraps it up, and folds her arms tighter.

She steps onto the porch, moving slowly, eyes never leaving mine. The wood creaks beneath her bare feet. She looks down at the damage, then at me, then at the bag.

"You think cinnamon and kindness are going to fix this or whatever we have going on?"

Her voice is even, but something flickers behind it. Something frayed at the edges.

I don't answer. Not yet. The wind's too sharp for a lie and too quiet for a full truth.

Instead, she exhales like she's surrendering to something. She lowers herself onto the top step—cautious, careful not out of fear the porch might give again, but like she's unsure what part of her will if she lets her guard down.

She pulls the paper bag toward her and peeks inside, lips twitching as the scent hits her. For a second, she just stares at it. Like it's too much and not enough all at once.

Then she takes the cinnamon roll out, peels back the wax paper with fingers that are steady only because she wills them to be.

"I haven't eaten since this morning," she says, almost to herself. "And that was half a granola bar and four espresso shots."

She tears off a piece and pops it in her mouth. Then another, she chews fast, like she needs the motion more than the taste. Like eating is the one decision she can still make without second-guessing it.

"Stress eating," she mumbles through a bite, wiping her thumb along the edge of her mouth. "Classic Jenna move."

I lean against the railing, watching her, unsure if stepping closer will break the moment or hold it in place.

"You don't have to explain it."

"I know," she says, swallowing. "But if I don't narrate my own chaos, it just... takes over."

There's no self-pity in it. Just honesty.

She keeps eating like it's buying her time. Like the cinnamon roll is the only thing grounding her to the porch, to me, to now.

And then, like a crack finally splintering through the surface she starts talking.

"I wasn't always like this," she says, eyes on the broken railing. "Or maybe I was, and I just didn't notice until other people did. That's the worst part, you know? When someone else points out your damage before you've even figured out where the cracks are."

She lets out a sharp breath and tears another piece off the roll, more aggressive this time.

"I talk too much when I'm anxious. Or I shut down. There's no in-between. I've ghosted landlords, therapists, entire zip codes. And not in the sexy, mysterious way. Just... poof. Gone."

She pops another bite into her mouth, chews fast, swallows hard.

"I once broke up with a guy because he reorganized my spice rack. Like alphabetically. I told him it was about autonomy and boundaries, but really? I just couldn't handle someone knowing where I kept my paprika without asking."

She laughs. It's short and brittle but there's no humor behind it, only the exposure. Only the feeling of someone who's been holding her breath for too damn long.

"I'm tired of being the flight risk or being the girl who people like until they realize I come with a warning label."

Her hand is still in the bag, but she's not eating anymore.

"I wanted to leave, JP, after the fire extinguisher thing. I packed up that night and I didn't even brush my hair. I just stood there, bag by the door, looking at this town like it was some test I already failed."

Her voice drops.

"But I didn't."

She finally looks at me.

"I stayed."

And that's when I know this isn't about the porch. It never was.

The confession hangs in the air between us, soft as breath, heavy as stone. For a moment, everything stills. Even the wind seems to pause. It's the kind of sentence you don't just say, you surrender it. And she just handed it over like a bruise still blooming.

But the moment doesn't hold.

CRACK.

The porch jerks beneath her. A split-second screech of wood giving way and then one of the boards buckles under her weight.

She stumbles with a sharp gasp, one leg plunging through the gap. I'm moving before I think, reaching for her but she yanks herself upright before I can get there, cheeks flushed, hands shaking. She brushes me off without touching me.

"Dammit," she spits, biting the word through clenched teeth. "Of course it falls apart. Of course it does."

She steps back, breath ragged, cinnamon roll forgotten behind her, cooling in the breeze like the rest of this night.

I watch her unravel not in fear, but in fury. And it's not the porch she's mad at.

"It's fine," she says tightly, flicking crumbs from her lap. "It's perfect, actually. Classic."

"Jenna—"

"No. Don't."

Her voice slices through mine, sharp and final. She won't meet my eyes now. She's too busy reassembling her armor piece by piece.

"Don't soften it. Don't offer some poetic line about how things fall apart to make room for something better. Just let it be broken. Let me be broken."

She turns before I can answer. Walks toward the door like she's walking away from something much deeper than old wood and rusted nails.

And just before she steps inside, she glances back once her eyes not soft, not pleading, just tired.

"I stayed," she says again, quieter this time. The words land differently now. Bitter at the edges. Fragile at the center. "That was my mistake."

The screen door creaks open.

Slams shut behind her.

And I'm left alone on a porch that can't hold weight I'm watching the last piece of her disappear into a house she never meant to belong to.

Chapter 9

Jenna

A couple weeks had passed and it seems as though Willow Cove had transformed overnight.

The Fall Festival took over the town with a kind of cheerful precision with every storefront trimmed in golden leaves, every lamp post wrapped in plaid ribbon and burlap bows. Main Street had become a slow-moving river of people and color, lined with vendor tents and hand-painted signs offering pumpkin bread, maple fudge, mulled cider, and knitted scarves that looked more decorative than warm.

Pumpkins crowded wooden crates in every shade imaginable from chalky white, ghostly blue to deep velvet orange. Cornstalks framed every doorway, hay bales became benches and from somewhere up near the town square, the sweet pulse of fiddle music lilted across the air, soft and familiar, like something from an old memory playing on repeat.

The breeze carried the scent of caramel apples and woodsmoke, mixing with crisp leaves and cinnamon sugar. Children shrieked as they tumbled through hay mazes near the courthouse steps, their cheeks flushed, faces painted in foxes and owls. Teenagers clustered around the cider truck, pretending not to care who was watching them. Everyone else seemed to be carrying a paper cup or a canvas tote. They had something warm, something homemade.

Overhead, strings of Edison bulbs zigzagged between buildings, glowing like trapped stars. The sky beyond them had gone pale and low, the kind of overcast that made colors look richer, deeper, like the whole town had been brushed in nostalgia and left to dry.

Willow Cove didn't just decorate for fall.

It became it.

The crowd thinned near the end of Main Street, where The Willow Bean Café sat tucked beneath a canopy of maple trees still holding onto their copper-bright leaves. The shop had gone full fall with a wreath on the door, hay bales stacked with plaid throw pillows, and a chalkboard sign perched out front that read:

"Pumpkin Spice & Puck-Sized Pumpkins — Carve, Sip, Stay Awhile."

That last part caught me.

Through the window, I spotted a long table set up near the back, covered in newspaper and surrounded by kids' elbow-deep in paint, markers, and pumpkin guts. A little chaos and a lot of glitter. One boy was stabbing his pumpkin with a carving tool like he was avenging something. Another girl was trying to glue yarn onto hers like it was a wig.

And in the middle of it all, perched on a stool with her legs crossed and a serious look of artistic concentration on her face it was Maisie.

She had a hockey puck clutched in one hand and a squat little pumpkin in the other, tongue sticking out the corner of her mouth as she carefully glued the puck to the pumpkin's front.

Beneath it, she was sketching stick legs with what looked like goalie pads.

My chest tightened.

I reached for the door handle before I could overthink it.

The bell chimed overhead as I stepped into the warmth of the café, the cider in the air, espresso in the walls, something sweet and cinnamon rising from the counter.

Maisie looked up first.

Her face lit like she'd been waiting for me all day.

"Miss Jenna!" she shouted, nearly dropping her pumpkin in her excitement. "You came!"

The café paused around her voice and just for a second then it moved on. But I didn't. I stood there like an idiot, hand still on the door, blinking at a kid who somehow managed to disarm me every single time.

"Hey, Maisie," I said, forcing a smile. "That's a pretty fierce-looking pumpkin."

She beamed and held it up proudly. "He's a goalie. I named him Puck Rogers. He's protecting the pumpkin patch from evil!" She turned him slightly. "See? I gave him knee pads and rage."

I laughed—actually laughed—and stepped closer.

"You give all your pumpkins battle plans?"

"Just the ones that deserve a storyline."

She shifted to make space beside her. "You wanna help me paint the next one? You can name it."

I hesitated. There was a dozen excuses already lined up in my head. I had things to do. I didn't want to intrude. I wasn't ready to feel things today.

But none of them made it past my throat.

So, I sat down next to her, and picked up a brush.

Maisie was halfway through explaining the final battle between Puck Rogers and the Evil Turnip King when the bell above the café door jingled again.

I didn't look up.

The Willow Bean had been a steady swirl of motion all morning with many people ducking in from the chill, laughing with warm drinks in their hands, brushing leaves from their jackets. I stayed focused on Maisie's pumpkin, on the glitter paint drying unevenly across its face. She had just handed me a marker with the solemnity of a general issuing orders, and I was under strict instructions to draw battle armor. I didn't mind if it gave my hands something to do.

But then I heard his voice.

Low, familiar and a little hoarse, like he hadn't meant to speak yet.

"Hey, Mace. Looks like you've got a goalie now."

I froze, the marker suspended mid-line.

Maisie lit up like a jack-o'-lantern at full wattage. "JP!" she squealed.

I looked up, slow and careful.

He stood just inside the doorway, shaking out the last mist of rain from his coat. A knit beanie hugged his dark hair, curls peeking out around the edges. His jacket was unzipped, hoodie visible beneath, the kind of casual layered look that probably wasn't intentional but still worked. Water dripped off his shoulders. His eyes were already on Maisie.

And then they found me.

Something shifted in his face; it wasn't a smile, not a flinch. Just... stillness, like a held breath. And for the briefest second, it felt like the last two weeks hadn't happened. Like I hadn't said too much and then pushed him away. Like we were still on that porch, seconds before everything fell apart.

Maisie launched herself toward him. He caught her midair, effortlessly, his hand spreading across her back like second nature.

"You should've seen it," she said as he set her down. "I gave him goalie pads and rage. Puck Rogers doesn't let anyone pass."

He chuckled, brushing a loose strand of hair from her forehead. "Sounds about right."

She beamed, and I found myself watching the way he looked at her and not with just fondness, but like she mattered. Like he saw all of her.

His gaze flicked back to me.

I offered a small smile. Civil. Contained. "We're starting the next one. Still figuring out its personality."

JP stepped closer to the table, eyes sliding down to the half-carved pumpkin in front of me. "Judging by the blade marks, I'd say chaotic-neutral."

A laugh caught in my throat, soft and involuntary.

It felt dangerous, this closeness. This ease. Like we were on the verge of something again. Like if we kept talking, we might slip back into whatever had been building before the porch splintered and I ran.

And then—

"Jon Paul?"

The voice behind him was glossy and cold, dipped in familiarity.

His whole body stiffened.

Mine did, too.

He turned before I could.

She was already stepping inside, framed by the open door like a memory that had learned how to dress better.

She was tall, flawless and effortless. Dressed in a camel coat and bone-colored boots. Lipstick the exact color of blood-orange tea. Her hair fell in those perfectly lazy waves women like me always suspected came with a personal stylist. Her smile was bright. Her eyes were not.

"Chelsea," JP said flatly.

She laughed like he'd just told a private joke. "Wow. It really is you."

Maisie took a tiny step closer to me. I didn't move.

"I heard you were back," Chelsea continued, sweeping a glance around the café like she was already bored with it. "Didn't think I'd see you here of all places. This town still makes its own soap, doesn't it?"

She reached out with a light touch on his arm, casual only if you didn't know better. "Still coaching?"

"Yeah," JP said, neutral. "Youth team."

"That's cute," she said, then glanced down at Maisie. "Is this your niece?"

"She's a friend," he replied, and there was something in the way he said it that sounded an awful lot like a warning.

Maisie blinked at her, then turned back to her pumpkin and began carving with the intense focus of someone trying to disappear into the act.

I picked up my own carving tool. My hands were steady, but something inside me wasn't.

Chelsea's eyes finally landed on me.

She didn't blink. Didn't smile.

Just took me in like I was a countertop that needed refinishing.

I nodded politely. "Hi."

She tilted her head. "And you are?"

"Jenna," I said evenly. "Maisie's carving partner."

"Adorable."

She turned back to JP. "Well. It's good to see you."

Her voice lingered a second too long on *good.*

And then, as quickly as she came, she was gone—turning on her spotless heels and vanishing out the door in a swirl of expensive perfume and unfinished tension.

The café quieted in a way only people who were pretending not to listen know how to do.

Maisie leaned over to me and whispered, "She looks like someone who irons her shoelaces."

And I nearly choked on a laugh.

But I didn't look at JP.

Not yet.

I just pressed my carving knife a little deeper into the pumpkin.

Sometimes silence is safer than what might slip out.

Maisie didn't notice the way the temperature had dropped around us. Her focus stayed locked on her pumpkin as she carefully painted tiny silver lightning bolts along the edges of the goalie pads. Her tongue poked out between her lips, her brow furrowed with pure concentration.

I forced my smile to stay in place.

"I'm going to get a napkin," I told her gently. "Back in a sec."

She nodded, already reaching for a new brush, completely unaware of the storm gathering a few feet behind her.

I turned and walked toward the back corner of the café, past the sugar-dusted pastries and steaming cider carafes, past the curated charm of the carved wooden signs and mason jar lights. My boots clicked quietly against the tile until I reached the far window, where no one was watching and the afternoon light spilled in gold through the glass.

I didn't have to look back to know he followed.

I could feel the weight of him long before he spoke.

He stopped a few feet behind me, close enough to speak low. "Jenna—"

I didn't turn. Not yet.

"You want to tell me what that was?" I asked, my voice quiet but deliberate, cutting straight to the bruise.

He hesitated. "That was Chelsea."

"I got that part."

"She's my ex," he said again, like repetition would soften the truth. "We ended it a long time ago."

I turned slowly, meeting his eyes with the steadiness I'd earned the hard way.

"What's 'a long time ago,' exactly?"

"Almost a year," he said. "Right before I moved back."

"And did she get the memo?" I asked, arms folding across my chest. "Because she looked pretty comfortable acting like you were still hers."

JP exhaled hard. "She doesn't matter anymore."

"She mattered enough to freeze you up the second she walked in the room."

His jaw flexed. "I didn't want to make a scene. Not in front of Maisie and not in front of you."

"That wasn't avoiding a scene," I said. "That was disappearing. I was sitting right there, and you made me feel like I didn't exist."

He stepped forward. Just a few inches. But it felt like a line he hadn't crossed in two weeks.

"You're not just someone to me, Jenna."

I held his gaze. "Then why did you act like I was invisible the moment your past showed up?"

His voice dropped lower, rougher. "Because I didn't know what to do. You're the first person who's made me feel like I want to try again. For real. And I didn't want to ruin it by saying the wrong thing."

I blinked. "So instead, you said nothing."

He ran a hand through his hair, frustrated. "I should've said something that night. On the porch. I should've stayed, or followed you, or just... told you the truth."

"What truth?"

"That I was scared," he said, and this time it wasn't defensive at all, it was raw.

"Of me?" I asked, even though I already knew.

"Of messing it up," he said. "Of letting someone in and not being enough. Of wanting more and losing it again."

I stood quiet for a moment, letting the words settle.

Letting him feel the space between them.

"I'm not asking you to be perfect, JP," I said, voice gentler now, but no less firm. "I'm asking you to show up. Not just when it's convenient. Not when it's safe. But when it counts."

"I'm trying."

"Then try harder."

His eyes flickered like he wanted to argue. But he didn't.

I took a step closer, enough that he'd hear every word.

"You want this?" I asked. "Then the next time someone like her shows up and talks like I'm nothing; you don't stand there and let it happen."

He opened his mouth. Closed it again.

"I've spent years convincing myself I don't take up space," I whispered. "Don't you dare help someone else erase me."

Then I stepped back. Slowly. Intentionally.

And before I can leave, JP makes the move to head towards the door first.

Not with a storm, not with a slammed door.

He just leaves, I look around watching as the small-town people stare, as the embarrassment creeps in. I grab my coat and make my way back to the cottage walking the long way around to avoid running into him.

Chapter 10

JP

The rink is too quiet.

No puck echo, no blades biting in. Just the hum of old fluorescent lights overhead and the low moan of the building settling into its bones. The kind of silence that feels built-in, layered beneath coats of paint and banners that haven't been touched since the last championship three seasons ago.

I glide out to center ice, alone. No stick. No gear. Just my boots scraping faint lines into the surface like I need to leave a mark, even if it's one that fades by morning. The air is sharp, metal-tinged. Familiar in the way a scar is—you don't feel it every second, but you never forget it's there.

And I don't hear the door. I feel it.

A subtle shift in the air, the kind that cuts through the ribs. Then the sound. The echo of boots that don't belong here. Thin heels tapping rubber matting with purpose. Rhythmic. Sharp. Deliberate.

I don't turn around.

"Jon Paul."

She says it's like the syllables taste expensive. Like I'm still hers, Jenna was right when she pointed it out.

I close my eyes for half a second. Inhale through my nose. Let the cold settle under my skin before I answer. "You always did know how to find me."

Chelsea laughs behind me—soft, polished, smug. It echoes in this space like perfume. "The rink always was your church. I figured you'd still worship here."

I turn. Slowly. Deliberately. Because some things don't deserve urgency.

She stands near the blue line in a coat that costs more than my monthly paycheck and boots that have never seen slush. Hair immaculate. Lipstick precise. Her smile is too white. Her eyes are too hollow.

"Didn't expect you to still be here honestly," she says. "Then again... loyalty was always your strongest trait."

I fold my arms, say nothing.

"You look good," she adds. Like it's a compliment. Like it costs her something.

"What do you want, Chelsea?"

Her smile falters just enough to show the edge beneath. Then she steps closer, letting her heels click like punctuation. "Maybe I made a mistake."

There it is. No apology. Just an implication. The ghost of regret without the weight of ownership.

I scoff, low in my chest. "That took you long enough."

"I'm not here to beg."

"You're not here to leave me alone either."

She crosses her arms. Leans into the stance like it's a pose she practiced. "You and I were good together. You know that."

I shake my head. "No, Chelsea. We were convenient. We were curated. You didn't love me. You loved how I looked standing next to you."

Something flashes across her face—surprise, maybe. Or guilt dressed in anger.

"You really think this little town can hold you?" she snaps. "That girl—"

"Don't."

One word. One syllable. Cold as the ice beneath us.

"You think she understands your world? That she can carry the weight of it? You think she won't crumble the second it gets hard?"

I step in, slow but close enough that she has to tip her chin up to meet my eyes.

"She already knows what hard looks like. And she didn't run."

Chelsea scoffs. "She doesn't know you. Not like I do."

"No," I agree, voice low. "She knows me better."

She stares, eyes narrowing. Her lips press into a tight line like she's trying not to break first. But she always does.

"You're making a mistake," she whispers.

"No," I say, and this time my voice doesn't shake. "I already made it. And I learned from it."

She swallows. Straightens. Adjusts her coat like armor.

"Goodbye, Chelsea."

I don't wait for her to speak again. I turn before she can find a new angle

I skate back to the center. Plant my boots. Tilt my head up toward the rafters. Let the cold burn through the last of the doubt.

She came to reclaim me.

But she never understood:

I was never hers to keep. I turn slightly with the corner of my eye. I see she's still standing there waiting for me to give in to her whims.

She adjusts her coat like its armor, but I see through the stitch-perfect confidence. That flick of her wrist, the tilt of her chin—it's all fabric and performance. The Chelsea I remember always knew how to curate herself for the moment. But what she doesn't know is that I've stopped being the kind of man who believes in her curtain calls, and I realize I haven't said my peace yet.

"You left without a word," I say, and it's not loud, but it lands hard. Like the first crack through a frozen pond. "You didn't just walk away from a relationship—you walked away from me. From the version of me who still believed people don't vanish when things get heavy."

Her mouth tenses, like she might interrupt, but I'm already in motion. Not with my feet—but with my voice. With the truth I've never said out loud, not even to myself.

"You disappeared," I continue, "and you did it in the exact way you knew would break me the cleanest. No text. No call. No goodbye. Just a week of silence that stretched into a month. A month that twisted into half a year. And by then? Everyone else had moved on. But I was still trying to figure out how I became something disposable."

She flinches just barely. But I see it. In the eyes. In the corners of her mouth.

"I buried that silence," I say, quieter now. "In locker rooms. In hotel walls. In the curve of a whisky glass, I never drank because I couldn't trust myself with it. And you—God, Chelsea—you just became a name people whispered when they didn't think I could hear."

She stands there like she wants to speak but doesn't know how to defend herself. Because there is no defense. Not for this.

"So why now?" I ask, and my voice is colder than the ice under us. "Why here? Why me?"

I pause. Just long enough to mean it.

"What makes me worth circling back to now?"

The words echo.

Not like a shout. But like a judgment.

She shifts her weight, but it's too late for theatrics. There's no camera crew here to reframe this moment. No scripted spin to clean it up in post.

"Was it the headlines drying up?" I ask, stepping in. "The endorsements are fading? Or just that I was always the easy one—the fallback plan who didn't yell when you left because he was too stunned to stand upright?"

Her eyes flash. She wants to be angry. That's her shield. But I don't let her pick up the sword this time.

"You came back because you thought I'd still be where you left me. Still holding the door open. Still stuck on page forty-seven of a story you had no intention of finishing."

I shake my head.

"You don't get to do that."

The silence between us is sharp now. Brittle.

She opens her mouth again—maybe to apologize, maybe to pretend none of it happened—but I cut her off with the truth.

"You made your choice, Chelsea. Not just once. Not in a moment of fear or confusion. You made it over and over again. Every time you didn't reach out. Every time you let someone else speak for you. Every time you saw my name in the news and didn't call."

My voice breaks on the edges. Just enough to sting. Just enough to feel like truth being pried out from bone.

"You don't get to knock on this door like it was never locked."

Her eyes glisten, but no tears fall. Chelsea Wilcox doesn't cry in public. She lets her damage leak out in subtler ways—tight shoulders, unspoken words, the way her hands tremble just once before stilling again.

I take a step back. Not in retreat. In refusal.

"You don't get to want me only after the world stops. After the spotlight shifted. After someone else started seeing me for who I really am."

I look at her one last time—this woman I once imagined a future with. And I don't feel hate. I don't even feel hurt.

I feel done.

Finished in the way a wound finally scabs over.

"I'm not here to be your soft place to land," I say quietly. "Not anymore."

And still, she says nothing.

Because there's nothing left to say.

She stands there, coat wrapped tight around her, and I wonder—for the first time—if this version of her ever really existed outside of my grief. Maybe she was always just a story I told myself. A dream I clung to so I wouldn't have to face how alone I really felt after the fall.

But that dream's gone now. I let it dissolve in the frost between us.

I turn. Not as a statement. Just a release.

And when I hear the door open behind me I hear her heels click their retreat—I don't look back.

She leaves.

And the silence that returns isn't cold.

It's clean and free of something I've held onto in the back of mind since she left.

I step out into the night, and for a second, I think I might finally be alone.

The air hits sharp. Clean. The kind of cold that clears the lungs but not the conscience. I keep my head down, hands jammed in my coat pockets as I cross the lot, the glow from the overhead lights casting long, skewed shadows across the slush-covered gravel. My breath puffs white into the dark like some kind of steam signal, trailing behind me while I pretend that what just happened inside doesn't matter.

But I know it does.

And she's waiting.

Jenna stands beside my truck, leaning against the passenger-side door like she owns the ground beneath her. Arms folded, legs crossed at the ankle, hair pulled back in a loose braid that's started to unravel in the breeze. Her coat's open, her cheeks pink from the cold, but her eyes are lit with something sharper than wind chill.

She doesn't flinch when I spot her. Doesn't pretend she's just passing by. She was waiting—for me.

Of course she was.

I stop walking, about ten feet away. She doesn't close the distance. She just looks at me. Not with anger, not even with frustration. Something worse.

Disappointment.

"You weren't going to call," she says. Her voice is calm. Unforgiving.

"No," I admit.

A beat. The kind that feels like a verdict.

She straightens, takes a step forward. Her boots crunch over the gravel, deliberate and slow, like she's pacing out the perimeter of her patience.

"Because disappearing after the café was easier?" she asks, eyebrows raised. "You left me in the middle of a sentence, JP. In front of half the town."

My jaw tightens. "I wasn't trying to hurt you."

"But you did."

Her words are stripped of theatrics. Just a fact. The kind that lands deep because they're said so plainly. Like gravity.

"I needed space," I say, voice tight.

"No. You needed to not be accountable. Big difference."

She delivers the line without heat. Without venom. Just the sharp edge of someone who's learned the cost of emotional exit wounds.

"You think walking out is better than staying messy?" she asks. "You think silence makes it noble?"

I rub my hand across my face, trying to steady the hurricane in my chest. She isn't yelling. That's what makes it worse. She's here. Calm. Brave. Saying everything I couldn't.

"I didn't want you to see me like that," I say quietly.

Her expression doesn't shift. "Like what?"

"Unraveled. Unsteady. I've spent the last year building some kind of life here, one step at a time, like a guy climbing out of a trench. Chelsea showing up felt like slipping straight back into the hole."

She nods. Just once. "So instead of reaching for someone, you chose to retreat. Again."

Then again that slices deep.

"I didn't know how to stay," I say. "Not with all that history crashing into the present."

Jenna folds her arms tighter. "You don't get to ghost real-time pain just because your past feels louder than I do."

The words come low, but they hit me like a puck to the ribs. No wind left.

She looks at me, really looks, like she's assessing whether I'm still worth this fight. Whether I'm more than an echo of someone who's always preparing to leave.

"I'm not asking you to be fixed," she says. "I'm asking you to be present. There's a difference."

I blink, slow. Let the cold sting the corners of my eyes.

"You're right," I say, voice thick. "You're completely right."

She doesn't soften. Not yet.

"I don't want to be the woman you come to when the ghosts get loud, JP. I want to be the one you stay with before they show up."

My hands curl into fists inside my coat pockets.

"You're not a rebound," I say. "You're not a placeholder. You're not a maybe."

Her gaze flickers, just slightly, as if she's daring herself to believe it.

"I'm scared," I admit, and that's the part I haven't said aloud. "That I'll ruin this before I even know how to hold it."

"Then stop holding it like it's breakable," she says softly. "It isn't. Not if you show up for it."

Silence falls between us. Not the kind that isolates. The kind that steadies. Grounds. Heals.

I take one step closer. Then another.

Her breath catches just slightly. But she doesn't move away.

"I'm here," I whisper.

"For now?"

"No. For real."

She doesn't smile. She doesn't kiss me. She just nods. And it feels bigger than either of those things.

Then she reaches out and slides her fingers into mine. No pressure. No drama. Just the simple act of choosing to stay.

And I hold on.

Because this, finally, is what it feels like to stay.

Her fingers find mine, and for a moment, everything around us goes still.

The wind slips past my collar. The rink groans softly behind us. But none of it registers. Just the weight of her touch—small, steady, impossibly patient. She doesn't speak. She doesn't press. She just holds my hand like she's holding space.

And maybe that's what undoes me.

"I was scared," I say.

The words come out rough. Scraped raw by everything I've swallowed and never said.

She looks up at me. Not wide-eyed. Not expectant. Just open. Ready.

"Scared of messing this up," I go on. "Of stepping wrong, saying too much, or not enough. Of pulling you into my mess and watching you regret it."

The sentence hangs there, visible in the breath between us.

"I've been the guy left behind before," I say. "I know what it feels like when something good slips through your hands because you weren't brave enough to hold it. Or worse—because you held it too tight."

She doesn't let go. Not even a little.

"I told myself I was protecting you," I admit. "By staying quiet. By backing off. But that was a lie. The truth is—I was protecting myself. From the chance that you'd see all of me and walk away."

I take a breath. Cold air, sharp in my lungs.

"I didn't think I was enough," I say. "Not for this. Not for you."

Her eyes glisten—not with tears, but with something deeper. Recognition. Understanding. Like she's heard every word in a language she already speaks.

"I kept thinking that if I stayed quiet, if I held myself at arm's length, I couldn't ruin it," I say. "But I was wrong. Silence isn't safe. It's just another kind of running."

She exhales, soft and steady, and her thumb brushes the side of my hand. It's the gentlest thing anyone's done to me in months.

"You're not too much," she says. "And you're not not enough."

I blink, but I don't look away.

"And you're not the only one scared," she adds.

There's a pause. Not heavy. Not tense. Just real.

"I'm scared too," she says. "But that doesn't mean we walk away. It means we learn how to stay."

The air shifts. Not warmer. But clearer.

"I don't want to lose this," I say. My voice drops to a whisper. "Not again."

"Then stop holding it like it's already gone."

The way she says it—it knocks the air out of me in the gentlest way possible. Like something being laid down instead of taken away.

And in that quiet, I realize something I hadn't allowed myself to believe until now.

She's not asking me to be perfect.

She's asking me to be here.

And for the first time, I think I finally can be.

She lets the silence stretch for a few seconds. Not to punish, but to make sure I hear the echo of what I just said. Every inch of it.

Her hand stays in mine, but her shoulders square. Her spine straightens. There is a shift in her posture—still soft, still open but rooted now in something fierce.

"I am not asking you to be perfect, JP," she says. Her voice is calm. Clear. Unshakeable.

My chest tightens, instinct bracing for impact.

"I am not looking for a flawless version of you," she continues. "I am not expecting you to always say the right thing or never get scared. That is not real. That is not love."

She steps in, just enough to close the space. Just enough to make sure I cannot retreat.

"But I am asking you to show up."

Her words thread between my ribs, slow and exact.

"I am asking you to stop vanishing when it counts. To stop treating your own pain like a permission slip to undo everything we have built."

I open my mouth, but she lifts a hand. Not to silence me. To finish her truth.

"I know you have been hurt. I know you have lost. I know you think you are broken in ways I cannot touch."

She swallows hard, but her voice holds steady.

"But do not you dare help someone else erase me."

The words hit clean, like truth without mercy.

She steps back just slightly, just enough to look at me full-on.

"I will not compete with ghosts, JP. I will not shrink to fit into someone else's shadow. If you are still carrying her—if you are still leaving space for the past to pull you under—then let me go now. Do not keep me here just to prove to yourself that you are still worth keeping."

She does not look away. Not for a second.

And for the first time, I see it.

Not just the hurt. Not just the fear.

The power.

Jenna is not asking me to stay for her.

She is asking me to stay with her.

As an equal. As a partner. As someone who chooses her fully or not at all.

"I am not someone's stand-in," she says. "I do not wait around to be picked. I show up, JP. I do not run. And I sure as hell do not beg."

The finality of it rings out across the parking lot like something sacred.

And suddenly, I understand exactly what I have been handed.

A choice.

Not between her and the past.

Between presence and absence. Between courage and the quiet exit, I have always taken when it mattered most.

And this time, I do not want to run.

I want to stay exactly where I am.

Because she is not asking for perfection.

She is asking for me.

We stand in a parking lot that feels like a stage at the end of a play no one wanted to finish.

The light overhead flickers once, buzzing faintly like it is just as tired of waiting as she is. Her hand is still in mine, but the warmth there is fading—not physically, but in the way, gravity fades when something starts to lift away.

She is not pulling back.

But something in her is already leaving.

I see it in her stillness. In the silence she wraps around herself like a coat she never wanted to wear. She is not punishing me. She is protecting herself from what comes next.

This silence—it is not the gentle kind. Not the kind that leaves room for reflection.

This silence is the kind that counts.

She looks at me, and everything about her expression says what she refuses to repeat. That the next few seconds will be the last ones where this choice is mine.

That whatever I say now, or fail to say, will live in her memory longer than any kiss or promise I ever gave her.

And I can feel myself standing still in a body that wants to run. Muscles locked. Jaw wired shut. I am full of things that want out, but none of them know how to land without breaking both of us.

She blinks slowly. Not dramatic. Not even emotional. Just patient in a way that hurts more than anger ever could.

This is your last chance to get it right.

Not her words. Her silence.

It hums louder than the wind through the trees. Louder than the engine cooling behind us. Louder than the past pressing against the back of my skull.

This is the moment where people stay. Or vanish.

And I have vanished before.

Too many times.

I try to speak. My mouth opens. But the words catch somewhere between instinct and fear, and all that comes out is breath.

She feels it. She knows.

Because I watch her eyes shift—not away from me, but *through* me. Like she is watching the version of me she hoped for slowly dissolves.

Like she is already filing this away under lessons, not futures.

And that is the moment I understand something terrible.

This silence is not empty.

It is her letting go of me while I am still standing in front of her.

Chapter 11
Jenna & JP

Jenna

Morning tastes like old fear. Bitter, breath-warmed, and too familiar.

I sit at the edge of my bed, one sock on, the other abandoned near the baseboard like it even gave up halfway through the day. Light filters in through the gauzy curtain, the kind of light that tries too hard to feel gentle. It lands on my sketchpad, open to nothing but a smear of pencil that was meant to be a window or a door or something with edges. I don't remember starting it. I definitely didn't finish it.

There's no text from him.

No knock. No note. No proof that anything I said cracked through whatever wall JP has wrapped around his heart like a second skin. I didn't expect fireworks. But I thought—maybe—he'd say something. Try. Flinch.

I pull on my hoodie, the one with paint stains on the sleeve and a ripped cuff. It smells like cedar and my old life. I like it better that way—less like the girl who waited for men to decide if she was enough.

The kettle whistles low in the kitchen, but I let it go until it clicks off on its own. I'm not in the mood to pour comfort into a mug and pretend it'll fix anything.

Instead, I curl up at the kitchen table with my legs folded under me and stare at the list I wrote last night. A real list. Black ink. Bullet points. As if I could control heartbreak by organizing it.

- You stood your ground.

- You didn't cry in front of him.

- You said what needed saying.

- You didn't beg.

That last one. I circle it three times until the paper thins.

Somewhere between fighting for myself and walking away, I lost track of whether this is strength or just another kind of self-sabotage. But I meant every word. And if he's as afraid of losing it all as he said—then where is he now?

The silence presses its hands around my shoulders, like a ghost trying to hold me still.

I get up anyway.

The town doesn't wait for heartbreak. There's mail to check, errands to run, the café to pass by and pretend I'm not hoping to see a familiar truck parked in front. I braid my hair too tight and lace my boots like I'm heading into a battle I can't name. Maybe I am.

By the time I'm halfway down the street, I've already drafted ten versions of what I'd say if he showed up. And twenty of what I'll pretend to feel if he doesn't.

I push open the door to The Willow Bean and smile at Miss Edie like nothing inside me is unraveling. She's making espresso like it's a spell. For a second, I almost ask her to cast one.

Then I see the corkboard.

And the space where his sketch used to be.

Gone.

Just like him.

JP

She meant every word.

That's the part I can't shake. Not the ultimatum. Not even the look in her eyes when she said it. But the certainty. The kind of calm you only find when the storms already swallowed you whole. She didn't raise her voice. Didn't cry. Didn't even flinch.

She just drew a line.

And now I can't stop staring at it.

The house is too quiet, even with the radio low and the smell of sawdust creeping through every window. I started sanding the edge of the porch again this morning. I've done the same beam twice. Not because it needed it—but because I needed it. The scrape of grit against grain feels like something I can control. The rest? Not so much.

I used to think showing up meant not leaving. Staying put. Keeping your head down and your promises quiet. But she's right. I've been here without really *being here*. For Maisie. For this town. For her.

I let silence stand in for effort.

I let fear dress up like protection.

And now I'm sanding a porch like it might give me answers.

Maisie's drawing in the grass again. She's wearing a hoodie that swallows her whole, her braid crooked like she did it herself. She looks up every so often, just to make sure I'm still here. I nod every time. Not big. Just enough. She doesn't need me to talk. She just needs me not to disappear.

So I don't.

I finish the first plank. Then the next. The rot near the edge is worse than I thought, but that doesn't stop me. I tear it out, down to the bones. That's what it's going to take—rip out the soft, broken pieces and start again. With better wood. Stronger lines.

I'll rebuild this porch.

And maybe, if I'm lucky, rebuild something else, too.

I don't text her. Not yet. I won't drop another promise into her lap without the work to back it. She's done being erased, and I don't blame her. So instead, I start showing up.

I take the early shift at the rink, even though it's hell on my back.

I help Maisie hang her sketch in the café again, even though my chest tightens when I walk in and see the space where mine used to be.

I fix the railing.

I repaint the stairs.

And I show up at the hardware store like its church, asking questions I should already know the answers to. The guy behind the counter gives me a look like he's not sure whether I'm building something or burying something. Maybe both.

But every screw I turn, every board I replace feels like a sentence in a language I'm finally learning to speak.

I don't know if she'll see any of it.

But I'm still here.

And this time, I'm not just standing still.

Jenna

I don't linger after my second cup.

The café starts to fill with the late-morning crowd—contractors ordering double shots, moms juggling sippy cups and oat milk lattes. Miss Edie catches my eye and gives me that look, the one that says more than words ever could. I nod, weakly. Then I grab my sketchpad, tuck it under my arm, and leave.

Outside, the sun is too bright. The kind of brightness that pretends it's warmth, but doesn't actually touch you.

I walk slowly. Past the bookstore. Past the florist. Through the stretch of sidewalk that still smells faintly of cinnamon from the fall festival. I take the long route home, hoping the extra steps might wear down the sharp edge of disappointment pressing into my ribs.

The sketch was still gone.

And if that's the end of it—then fine. I said what I needed to say. I didn't ask him to be perfect. I asked him to show up. And maybe silence is still his answer.

But when I round the last corner and see my house, I stop short.

My porch.

The one I teased in a sticky note. The one that's been leaning since before I moved in, like it was tired of being overlooked. The one I learned to step over carefully, avoiding the soft board at the edge.

It's different.

The railing is new. The stairs have been sanded smooth. That bottom step—the one that used to creak like it held a grudge is gone, replaced with clean, solid wood. There's no brush. No tools. No fanfare.

Just the work. Quiet and done.

My heart hits hard, like it's trying to punch its way out of my ribs.

Because this isn't his porch. It's mine.

He crossed that line. He came onto my property, fixed something I'd accepted as broken, and left nothing behind but proof that he was here. That he listened. That he's trying.

And the worst part is—it works.

This isn't a gesture. It's not romantic or flashy or meant to be admired. It's just effort. Quiet, steady, unannounced. And that scares me more than any apology ever could.

Because now I have to decide what to do with a man who finally understands the difference between staying and *showing up*.

I climb the new stairs slowly. They don't groan under my weight. They don't flinch.

Inside, I set my sketchpad on the desk and take a long breath. The studio smells like coffee and cedar and the kind of glue that never quite dries. The rebrand waits for me. Sketches half-pinned to the wall. Color palettes curling at the corners. Notes scribbled in the margins like a version of me was trying to speak before I knew what I wanted to say.

His voice echoes anyway.

"You build from the inside out."

So I begin again.

Not with the logo. Not with the pitch. But with the bones. The truth. The why.

And every few minutes, I glance toward the window.

The brush is gone. The mess is cleared.

But the railing?

Still there.

Fresh. Steady. Waiting.

I turn back to my desk, heart steadying for the first time in hours—until I hear it.

Three knocks.

Sharp. Intentional. On *my* front door.

I freeze, pencil hovering above the page.

Because part of me already knows.

It's him.

Chapter 12

JP

I don't expect her to answer right away.

The knock still echoes behind my ribs, louder than it sounded against the door. My hand falls to my side, but I don't move. I just wait. That's something I'm learning—to stand still, even when it would be easier to leave.

There's movement inside. A pause. Then the soft click of a lock turning, the hush of the knob twisting, and the door opens just enough for her to appear.

Jenna.

Hair tied up, sleeves pushed to her elbows, pencil still behind her ear like she didn't mean to stop working. Her eyes meet mine—clear, steady, unreadable. She doesn't look surprised. She doesn't look mad either. She just looks... braced.

"I didn't know if you'd be home," I say.

"You knocked anyway."

I nod. "Yeah."

She leans against the doorframe. Doesn't invite me in. Doesn't shut me out. Just holds the space between us like she's not sure what it's for yet.

"Can I come in?"

A quiet stretch of silence passes between us. Not cold. Not warm either. Just real.

"You already did," she says softly. "This morning. With a hammer."

I blink. Then something like a smile edges into my voice.

"I figured the porch was safer than words."

Something flickers across her face—maybe surprise. Maybe something else she doesn't want to show me yet.

"You here to patch the roof too," she asks, voice steady as glass, "or just fix the things that don't talk back?"

I absorb it. Let it land. The sharpness doesn't sting—it steadies me.

"No roof work today," I say evenly. "Figured I'd try using words."

Her brow lifts, unimpressed. "Ambitious."

"Trying something new," I admit.

Still, she doesn't move.

She studies me the way a sculptor might study a flawed block of marble—carefully, critically, deciding whether it's worth the effort to keep carving or just leave it cracked.

"You're not coming in to justify silence," she says. "I'm not interested in polished apologies."

"Good," I answer. "I didn't bring one."

That earns a pause. Not approval. Not quite permission. But something.

She exhales, slow and measured, as if the act of opening the door might cost her something she's not sure I deserve.

Then without ceremony she steps back just enough.

"Kitchen," she says. "Don't sit. Don't touch anything."

"Understood."

And I cross the threshold like it matters.

Because it does.

We move slowly down the hallway to the kitchen.

I feel the warmth of the kitchen, all the decorations, drawings and aesthetics but she feels like a polar bear eating an ice cream cone.

She moves ahead of me, wordless, her steps efficient, precise. The air hums with the faint scent of coffee grounds and something citrus that clings to the edges of the counter. She doesn't offer me a seat. Doesn't ask if I want anything. She just stands by the sink; arms folded across her chest like a barrier she has no intention of lowering.

The folder's already on the table. Its presence feels intentional—like a placeholder for whatever conversation she's bracing to cut short.

"I wasn't sure if this was a conversation kind of day," I offer, careful not to soften my voice too much. She'd hear that and call it manipulation.

She doesn't look up. "Depends on what kind of conversation."

"The honest kind."

She lets that sit in the air between us. Then: "You've got about five minutes before I decide it's not worth the trouble."

I nod. "Fair."

I lean against the counter—not close, not casual. Just... present. I don't fill the space with nervous energy. I don't reach for small talk. I let her choose the pace.

"I came because I meant what I said last night," I tell her. "That porch wasn't a peace offering. It was a place to start."

She turns her head just slightly. "You think fixing a few boards means you understand how to rebuild trust?"

"No," I say plainly. "But I think doing something with my hands was the only honest thing I knew how to do without messing it up."

She meets my eyes now, and there's steel in hers.

"That's the problem, JP. You think effort and intimacy are the same thing."

I swallow that. Let it hit. She's not wrong.

"I'm not here to pretend like I've got it figured out. But I am here. And I want to stay in the room when it gets hard."

"That's a promise?" she asks.

"No," I say. "It's practice."

She blinks. But she doesn't soften.

She walks to the table, pulls out a chair, *her* chair and sits. She doesn't invite me to do the same.

"I've got a meeting to prep for and a business to rebrand," she says, flipping the folder open. "If you're still trying to be part of this, you'll be at the rink tomorrow. Eleven sharp."

"I will."

Her eyes flick to the window, like she's already somewhere else.

"You can let yourself out."

I don't argue.

I nod once, pick up the folder, and head for the door without asking for anything more.

Because she's not done being angry.

And I haven't earned the right to ask her not to be.

I step outside, folder in hand.

The door clicks shut behind me—not slammed, not slow. Just final enough to tell me I've still got work to do. The air bites colder than it did when I arrived. Or maybe that's just her still clinging to me.

I start down the steps I repaired with my own hands, every board now carrying the weight of everything I didn't get to say.

Halfway down the walk, I hear the door unlock again.

I turn.

She doesn't step out.

But something flutters through the air—paper, loose, scribbled, folding in on itself as it floats to the ground.

I catch it.

A sticky note.

Old. Curled at the corners. Just three words, written in black ink that's slightly smudged:

"Don't disappear again."

Chapter 13

Jenna

The parking lot outside the rink hasn't changed.

Cracks still vein across the asphalt like a map of missed repairs. A lone pine tree leans into the wind near the entrance, bending the same way I did when I first got here—quietly, carefully, hoping not to snap.

But I'm not the same as I was last week.

I sit in the car with the engine off, the heater ticking down as the interior cools. My fingers rest lightly on the wheel, not gripping it, not letting go. The silence inside the car is different now—no longer about escape, but about what's waiting.

In the side pocket of my bag, pressed between brand mood boards and strategy notes, is the tension I haven't named aloud. Not the work. The weight.

The memory of yesterday's cold kitchen and everything unspoken in it.

And the note.

Don't disappear again.

I don't know if he read it. If it mattered. I didn't wait to find out. I just let it fall and closed the door before I could lose my nerve.

It wasn't meant to be clever. Or cruel. It was an anchor—dropped between what was and what might still be.

I step out into the cold, breath sharp in my throat. I adjust the scarf around my neck and cross the lot with the kind of practiced calm that looks like confidence from the outside.

Inside, the rink is the same industrial hum as always with old metal beams, scuffed vinyl tiles, the faint echo of blades on ice and a whistle in the distance. Familiar, functional, cold.

I nod to Rachel at the front desk. She gives me a warm smile that doesn't reach her eyes. Not because she's unfriendly, but because everyone's watching now. Everyone knows something shifted, and no one's saying it out loud.

The meeting room is down the back corridor, just past the weight room. I walk slowly, not out of hesitation—but because I don't trust my face yet. Not to betray anything I've worked too hard to hold steady.

Voices drift under the door. Coach Daniels. Someone from facilities. A low laugh I don't recognize.

And then his voice.

Measured. Professional. Like nothing happened at all.

Of course he's already here.

I pause with my hand on the doorknob. The air feels colder here. Not because of the rink. Because of what I know is on the other side.

He's not going to disappear this time.

But that doesn't mean I'm ready to let him stay.

I square my shoulders. Pull the strap of my bag higher.

And I walk in like I own the place.

The conference room smells like old coffee and printer paper.

Chairs scrape lightly as people settle in—Coach Daniels at the end of the table, Rachel with her laptop open, and two assistant coaches flipping through early reports they won't reference again. There's a plate of muffins no one touches, and a whiteboard someone forgot to erase from a youth skills meeting earlier in the week. The phrase *"skate like it's personal"* is still scrawled across the top in blue marker.

It is personal. More than they know.

I spot him instantly.

JP's at the far side of the table, already seated, posture easy but alert. He looks up the moment I enter. Just a flick of his gaze, no nod, no smile. He doesn't speak. He doesn't need to. Him being here before I was, already said enough.

I keep my steps calm and steady, moving to the front of the room where the monitor is set up and the draft boards are already arranged.

...The folder I built now feels heavier under my hand, though nothing's changed on the page. I place my folder down. Flip it open.

I keep my shoulders straight. My voice steady.

But it's not lost on me that for a room full of people asking for vision, they're doing a remarkable job of resisting the lens.

"All right," I say, projecting without sounding sharp. "Let's get started."

Chairs shift again. A few people straighten. Rachel types something quietly. JP doesn't move.

"I've compiled feedback from the community engagement surveys, previous donor events, and player interviews. Most of it was consistent—clear tone, strong team values but one thing stood out across the board." I pause. Let the room lean in a little.

"No one's quite sure who you are off the ice."

One of the coaches frowns slightly. "We're a team."

"You are," I agree. "But branding isn't just about slogans or colors. It's about clarity. About trust. If the public doesn't know what you stand for beyond the rink, they'll never stand behind you."

I click to the next slide on the monitor—core values. Not mine. Theirs. Pulled from messy answers, half-formed phrases in exit interviews, players stumbling their way toward honesty.

And then I hear it—quiet, but clear.

"Keep going," JP says.

I glance up. He's still in his seat, still composed, but his attention is sharper now. Focused. Like he's not just hearing me he's listening.

So I do.

"Authenticity. Growth. Community. Accountability," I read. "These came up again and again, but they're not showing up in your visuals, your voice, or your outreach. You're asking people to support something they can't quite define. That changes today."

A murmur runs down the table. The coaches lean back in their chairs. Rachel's typing faster.

JP doesn't move.

But I see it in his eyes, he knows this isn't just about branding anymore.

It never was.

The proposal sits open in front of them, carefully laid out, page by page.

I've walked them through identity statements, culture gaps, the chasm between perception and presence. I've used their words, their metrics, their language. And still, I can feel it building.

Doubt, under the table. Resistance, dressed as formality. Questions, waiting like teeth.

And then—

His voice.

"Let me ask you something," JP says, not loud, not aggressive but pointed.

I look up. He's leaning back in his chair, arms crossed loosely, eyes fixed on mine.

"Are you here to build something new," he asks, "or just to fix what you think we broke?"

The room stills.

It's not the question. It's the way he asks it like he already knows what lives under my skin and wants to see if I'll bleed on cue.

There's no warmth in his voice. Just calm. Controlled.

Calculated.

And I feel it—fire rising sharp in my chest, not from offense but *recognition*.

He could have said anything.

But he chose the one thing that makes me reach for ice.

So I give it to him.

"I'm here because no one inside this room could tell the truth without losing something first."

My voice is even. Frosted. Not unkind. Just surgical.

"And because what you broke," I continue, looking straight at him, "isn't mine to fix. It's yours. I'm just the one holding up the mirror."

Silence.

He doesn't blink. Doesn't flinch. Just absorbs it like he expected that burn and needed to feel the cold anyway.

And then, for the first time since I entered the room, the power shifts.

Not in my favor.

Just... back to center.

I don't answer right away.

Because answers like this with truth like this—deserve silence first. Space to stretch. Space to *unsettle.*

So I let the pause breathe.

Let it press into the room like altitude.

I want them to feel what it's like to sit in the gap between certainty and consequence—the very space this team has spent years painting over with nostalgia and headlines and half-formed mission statements no one actually believes in.

Then I look at him.

JP.

Not gently.

Not cautiously.

Just... straight through.

Like I see the fuse he lit and know exactly how long it will take to reach the charge.

"You keep talking like this is about identity," I say, my voice quiet, crisp, and sharpened to a single point. "But it's not."

The sentence lands.

Every head turns.

Everybody shifts.

Eyes snap toward me and not because I raised my voice, but because I stopped pretending.

"It's about memory."

I step forward.

Not for effect. Not for control.

Because the weight of what I'm about to say requires *presence*.

"This team was built on a legacy you keep romanticizing but no one here has had the courage to take responsibility for what came after. You want loyalty without transparency. You want evolution without disruption. You want the respect of a rebuilt empire without admitting you burned the first one down."

My voice doesn't rise.

It sharpens.

Cold, deliberate, surgically measured.

"And that's why you're stalled. Because deep down, you think a logo refresh will erase the rot. You think rewriting the tagline will distract us from the fact that the culture hasn't changed—just the lighting."

I let it sit.

Let the silence shift into something dense.

And then—

I finish it.

"You don't need a rebrand," I say, each word falling like a verdict. "You need a reckoning. You need to stop polishing the rust and pretending it's gold."

The silence that follows doesn't just fall.

It *detonates*.

A stillness so complete it steals the breath from the room. The hum of the fluorescent lights becomes deafening. No one moves. No one blinks.

Because they heard it.

Not in the words.

In the *truth* they couldn't unsee once I said it out loud.

And I'm not finished.

Not until it's carved in the walls.

"And if you can't face that?" I tilt my head, the faintest shift. Controlled. Contained. "Then no brand in the world will save you. Not mine. Not yours. Not anyone's."

Coach Daniels leans back slowly, as if trying to find the edge of the seat beneath him.

Rachel's fingers go still above her keys, suspended in mid-air.

Even Benji—the most irreverent person in the building—doesn't speak.

And JP—

JP is undone.

Not obviously.

Not dramatically.

But I see it in the fraction of movement—the way his jaw flexes, like he's bracing for something he didn't expect to feel. The catch in his breath. The heat that flickers behind his gaze like a match scraped once, then held too close to the kindling.

It's not anger.

It's not admiration.

It's a want.

Raw. Unsparing. Unmistakable.

Like he just realized that the woman across the room didn't come to play nice—

She came to burn it all down and build something better from the bones.

He swallows hard.

And that's when I know I've got him.

Not just thinking.

Lit.

And then—just when the silence is stretched so tight it could snap—

Benji exhales.

Low. Slow. Reverent.

"Holy hell," he mutters, like someone just saw proof of divinity and lived to report it. "I'd like to formally nominate Miss Monroe as our new religion."

No one laughs.

No one even breathes.

Because when fire speaks in ice—

You listen.

I let the silence stretch one second longer.

Then I move.

No rush. No apology. Just precision.

I gather my materials with the same care I brought into the room—stacking each page, sliding each board, like nothing about what just happened shook me. Because it didn't.

I don't need agreement.

I don't need permission.

I built the truth and set it on the table. Whether they're brave enough to claim it is no longer my concern.

I tuck the folder under my arm. Adjust the strap of my bag.

And when I finally speak, it's not a challenge.

It's an invitation.

Cool. Unshaken. Final.

"When you're ready to begin…" I let my eyes flick across the table—Coach. Rachel. JP, still quiet. "…you have my number."

Then I turn and walk out.

And not a single chair dares to scrape behind me.

Chapter 14

JP

The road home unspools in shadows and quiet—just the low hum of tires against damp asphalt and the kind of silence that sinks into the bones.

I don't turn on music.

I don't make calls.

I drive like I'm still inside that room; her voice etched in my chest like a brand no one else can see.

By the time I crest the final hill and my house comes into view, the sky's dropped into that deep indigo haze that feels more like velvet than night. The porch light's already on—automatic, routine, unthinking.

But nothing about what's waiting for me is routine.

Because she's there.

Jenna.

Sitting on my porch like she's always belonged there.

One leg crossed over the other, posture straight but not stiff, a folder balanced on her thigh like a statement. Not clutched. Not forgotten. Just... there. Like it always knew where it needed to be.

She doesn't check her phone.

Doesn't glance up when the headlights wash across her.

She just waits.

Still. Calm. Unshakable.

Like the porch isn't mine anymore—but hers.

Like she came to *watch* what I would do next, not to *ask* for anything.

I sit in the truck for a second longer than I should, engine ticking in the cold. My hands stay on the wheel.

Because that's what she does to me she makes me still in ways I don't know how to be.

Everything that happened in that conference room is still humming under my skin. The silence she commanded. The fire buried in her ice. The precision of every word. She didn't present a brand.

She laid down a map of reckoning.

And now, without calling. Without warning. Without a single false note—

She's here.

On my porch.

Not waiting for me.

Waiting on me.

I kill the engine. Open the door. Step out like the gravel underfoot has never heard me walk like this before—slow, aware, half-certain the ground might shift beneath me.

She lifts her head then. No smile. No hello. Just those eyes, steady and impossible to ignore.

I don't need to ask why she came.

Because the answer's written in the stillness between us.

She came to see if I'd show up.

Not in that room.

Here.

Now.

She watches me approach, but doesn't move. Doesn't flinch. Just track my steps like each one means something.

And it does.

I stop a few feet from her, the porch boards groaning under my weight, loud in the hush of whatever this is. We don't speak for a moment. Just stand in it.

The distance.

The damage.

The fact that we've both survived the same wreck, but walked out carrying different pieces of it.

"I thought you'd say something after the meeting," she says finally, voice quiet but unsparing.

Not soft.

Not cruel.

Just weighted. Like the words cost something to hold.

I nod once, slowly. "I didn't think I should be the first to speak."

"Why?" Her tone sharpens slightly. "Because it was my fire, or because you were too afraid to name what it lit in you?"

I blink.

Because it's not just a question.

It's the truth, thrown like a gauntlet.

I exhale. "I didn't think I had the right."

"Why not?"

"Because I'm the one who disappeared the first time," I say, voice low. "Because you stood in that room and named every broken thing and didn't flinch while the rest of us stayed silent. Because what you said—what you *were*—was bigger than anything I've been brave enough to be."

The wind cuts between us, sharp but not cruel.

She steps closer, just enough that I feel her heat but not her forgiveness.

"I didn't come here for your guilt, JP," she says. "I came to see if you were done hiding behind it."

That lands hard. Too hard.

I run a hand across my jaw. "You tore that room apart, Jenna. I've never seen anyone do what you did. Not with that kind of clarity."

"I didn't go there to tear it apart," she says. "I went to finally say something without apology."

I look at her.

And I know, I've never wanted anything more than I want to *deserve this version of her.*

"And now?" I ask, breath catching. "What are you doing here?"

She doesn't hesitate.

"I'm here because I lit the match. But you're the one who decides if we rebuild or stand in the ashes."

My throat tightens.

Because it's not a metaphor.

It's the moment everything pivots.

She is not asking me to rescue anything.

She is offering me the one thing I never knew I could earn back, a place in her presence.

If I can carry the weight of it.

If I can stop pretending to be half-finished just because it feels safer than building something whole.

I step forward.

One more board creaks beneath me.

And I look at her but not like she's fragile.

But like she's the future.

And the fault line.

The porch groans beneath my boots as I take the final step, and I swear the air between us contracts.

She stands there like a match about to be struck her shoulders back, chin high, not flinching.

But I'm done circling her flame like it'll scorch me if I get too close.

Because the truth?

I want to burn.

I want to take every inch of that steel spine and fire-forged clarity and feel it against my skin—not just the brilliance of her mind, but the heat of her choosing. Choosing to show up. Choosing to wait here. Choosing me.

"You want to know what happened today?" I ask, my voice low, deliberate—each word coiled with purpose.

"You walked into that room and made gods out of ash. You didn't ask to be heard. You made silence a stage. You cracked every weak wall we were hiding behind and somehow, you did it without raising your voice."

She says nothing, but her breath isn't steady anymore.

Good.

"I watched men twice your age and half your worth blink like they forgot how to breathe. I watched a program bend but not because you forced it, but because they recognized power when it walked in wearing heels and a folder instead of armor."

My chest rises once, hard.

"I didn't speak because I've never seen anything that honest and that beautiful stand in the same body. And it scared the hell out of me."

That gets her.

Her lashes flicker. Her throat tightens. But she holds.

So do I.

"Jenna, I've spent every day since I met you trying not to want too much. But standing here, now? I want it all. The fire, the fear, the fallout. I want the part of you that no one else gets close enough to carry. And I'm done apologizing for that."

I step closer, slow and steady, until there's no air left between us.

No misunderstanding.

No going back.

"I don't want easy," I say. "I want you. Just like this."

The silence after my words hangs between us like breath before a storm—thick, charged, waiting for the strike.

And then—

She moves.

Not with hesitation. Not with caution.

But with a kind of reclaiming that makes my pulse detonate.

Her hand drops the folder.

It hits the porch like a discarded shield; there's no crash, no drama. Just finality. Like she's done defending herself from me.

And then she steps into me.

Fast. Full.

One hand fists in the front of my shirt, the other pressed flat against my chest like she's not just touching me—she's checking if I can hold the force of what's coming.

And then she lets it out.

"You want the fire?" she says, voice low, razor-sharp. "You think you've seen it?"

Her breath ghosts against my throat.

"You haven't even tasted the first spark."

Her eyes are molten. Wild. And absolutely clear.

"You want to know what I am, JP?"

Her voice is low. Dangerous. Not from anger but from power too long unclaimed.

"They didn't know what to do with my fire, so they called it too much. Too loud. Too angry. So I stopped burning for them. Let it die out on purpose. What came next wasn't silence—it was frost.

I became cold, calculated. A fortress no one could reach.

Not because I stopped feeling. But because I felt *too much*.

I became chaos to myself, sealed it in, iced it over. And in the quiet, I realized... they never wanted less of me. They just couldn't hold what I refused to drop."

Finally, something snapped me back to a version of myself that was long forgotten...

"You think what I did in that boardroom was fire? That was *nothing.* That was me keeping the burn contained. That was me still trying to fit inside the frame someone else built for me."

She steps in closer, and I swear to God, the heat rolls off her in waves. Not figurative. Not imagined.

She's radiating.

"I've spent my whole life being told to hold back. To edit. To wait my turn. To be palatable enough to stay in the room, but not loud enough to change it."

Her breath shudders but not from weakness, but from momentum.

Her other hand presses flat against my chest, right over my heart. Like a mark.

"But not anymore."

She meets my eyes and it's not a look.

"I am the woman who watched her own fire get doused one demand at a time—and now, I'm done asking for permission to light the match."

My lungs tighten. My vision blurs. Because this—

This is a rebirth in real time.

"I didn't come here to be saved," she says, voice lowering. "I came here to see if you could stand in the heat."

And then she leans in.

So close her breath is on my lips, and the whole world folds down to this one moment, this one edge of space between us.

Her voice drops to a whisper but it hits like thunder.

"Because if you can't, don't reach for me again."

And then she moves in swiftly, she kisses me. It's hard but decisive.

Like she just set herself on fire and dared me to do the same.

Chapter 15

Jenna

Morning comes without asking. There is no warmth, no softness to ease me into the day. Just a low, leaden sky pressing against the windows, heavy with the kind of gray that doesn't promise rain, only weight. Light filters in slowly, colorless and cool, stretching across the hardwood like a question I haven't decided how to answer.

I sit at the kitchen table in an oversized sweatshirt; hair still damp from a too-hot shower I barely remember taking. The coffee in my mug has gone lukewarm, untouched. My fingers rest around it anyway, as if heat through ceramic could anchor me to something solid. The house is still. Not peaceful. Hollow. Like it knows something came undone last night and doesn't want to speak too loudly about it.

And it did. Something broke open.

Because I kissed him.

Or maybe he kissed me.

Or maybe the moment did it for us and pushed us together like a fuse finally tired of waiting for a match.

Either way, I let it happen. I wanted it to happen. And it wasn't gentle.

It was the kind of kiss that rewrites memory. Not the ones we tell people about, but the ones that brand themselves into muscle and bone. The kind of kiss that speaks in a language older than fear. One that doesn't ask for permission or pretend to be safe. It knew what it was, and it didn't apologize. And I didn't flinch.

I close my eyes, and it all floods back in full detail. The porch light turns his hair to gold. The porch boards groaning beneath my step. The air crackling with what had lived between us for weeks but had finally outgrown its leash. The sound his breath made when I let go of the last piece of myself, I had kept hidden. And the way his hands didn't grab or claim. They steadied. They met me. They held space for the wildfire.

What I gave him in that kiss was not affection.

It was a revelation.

It was the truth of me, unarmored.

Not the Jenna I show at meetings or in mockups or while curating the kind of polite brilliance clients like to buy into. Not the Jenna who smiles in the right tone or answers with wit before anyone realizes she's bleeding under the charm. Last night, I didn't offer any of that.

I offered the storm.

And he kissed it like he wanted to drown.

I eventually move. My legs stretch out from under the table, bare feet hitting the cool floor as I cross the room and flick on the studio light. The soft amber glow settles across my drafting desk like an invitation.

I don't need a reason today. No brief. No deadline. Just the ache in my hands to make something that isn't wrapped in compromise.

I settle into the desk and lower the pencil again, letting the weight of it guide me back into the silence. My hand finds the page without effort this time. Not tentative. Not restrained.

The lines come faster.

Broader strokes. A deeper lean in the figure's spine. The shoulders angled like they've just weathered something and haven't yet stood upright again.

I draw breath as I draw limbs that are arched, deliberate, coiled with something that feels like consequence. The body is male now. The presence is unmistakable. Broad across the chest. Grounded through the hips. One hand clenched at his side, the other not quite reaching for anything.

I don't stop to question it.

I just keep going.

The eyes stay unfinished, because I know if I try to draw them, I'll get lost. Not yet. Not when my hands still remember how his chest rose under my palm. How he looked at me like I had just turned gravity inside out and dared him to stay standing.

The figure isn't JP. Not exactly.

But it carries the memory of him. The weight of that kiss. The heat of his confession. The restraint in his hands and the fire in his voice when he finally said he wanted all of me without apology, without flinching.

My heart pounds harder the longer I draw.

It's not the image that wrecks me.

It's the realization that this is how I know I meant it.

That when I kissed him, it wasn't a performance. It wasn't about proving power or making a point.

It was about coming home to a part of myself I had spent too long keeping quiet.

The sketch stops being composition. It is starting to be a release.

Shadow under the jaw. The line of a neck bent in thought. A spine caught between tension and surrender. I don't even know what he's doing anymore. I just know what he feels like to look at.

Like risk.

Like relief.

Like ruin I'm not afraid of anymore.

My hand finally stills. The pencil drops to the desk, rolling to a quiet stop.

I lean back and stare at what I've made.

It's not polished. It's not pretty.

But it's true.

And that's enough.

My hand finally goes still, the pencil resting against the page like it, too, has nothing left to release. The sketch stares back at me, unfinished but unafraid—lines that tremble slightly, strokes that push too hard in places, but somehow it breathes. Somehow, it speaks.

It is not polished. It is not symmetrical.

But it is true.

And today, that is enough.

I let my fingertips graze the edge of the shoulder I just shaped, smudging the charcoal with the soft pad of my finger. I don't fix it. I don't sharpen the line or cover the imperfection. I let it stay—rough, honest, uncontained.

This is not about presentation.

It's about proof.

Proof that what happened last night didn't unravel me. Proof that I am still here, steady in my bones, and no longer asking for permission to take up this kind of space. Proof that I can want, and feel, and burn, and not lose myself in the wanting.

I close the sketchbook slowly, carefully folding the moment back into silence. The page creases at the edge, but I let it. The weight of it feels earned.

Then I lean back in the chair and inhale a full breath. Not sharp. Not shattered. Just a breath.

Grounded. Whole.

And that's when the phone rings.

The phone buzzes again, dragging across the counter with an insistent rattle that breaks through the quiet like a stone through glass. I glance at it, my thumb resting just above the screen.

Same number. Local. Still unknown.

I don't answer immediately.

Instead, I study the glow. Let it vibrate once. Then twice. I roll my shoulders back. The weight of the sketch still lingers on my fingertips, the charcoal smudge drying faintly along the edge of my hand like evidence.

When I finally swipe to answer, my voice is calm. Controlled.

"This is Jenna."

A pause. Half a breath, maybe. Then the voice clicks in. Male. Late thirties, maybe forties. Quick cadence, but carefully modulated. The kind of voice that's used to being listened to.

"Hi. Jenna Monroe? This is Mike from player development over at the rink."

I don't say anything.

He fills the space like he expected that.

"Your proposal stirred up a lot of conversation yesterday. Some folks were surprised by how bold it was. A few weren't thrilled. But no one could stop talking about it."

I let him go on.

"Couple of the team guys, leadership and players asked to meet. Nothing formal. They just want a sit-down, talk through a few concerns. Maybe get clarity on some of the shifts you're suggesting."

He pauses here, gauging me through the silence. I picture him with one hand on a clipboard, glancing at the time, unsure if I'm going to play nice or scorch the call into memory.

"You available around three this afternoon?"

Still, I don't speak.

I watch a trail of light move across the countertop from the window behind me. The second cup of coffee I poured still sits untouched beside my sketchbook. The house holds its breath like it knows this matters.

And then I speak.

"I'm available."

Simple. Direct.

But he keeps going.

"Great. I appreciate it. Should be pretty straightforward. Some of the guys are skeptical, but it's nothing you can't handle, I'm sure."

That's the moment I decide to let the match touch the edge.

"If they have real questions," I say, voice even, "I'll bring real answers. But if they're hoping I'll play translator for their discomfort, I'll save everyone the time and walk out early."

The line quiets. Just for a second. I can almost hear him recalibrating.

Then a low laugh hums through the speaker. Not patronizing. Impressed.

"Well. Message received."

He clears his throat.

"See you at three, then."

The line goes dead.

I set the phone down slowly. Let it rest on the counter as I return to the stool, hand still warm from the call. I look at the sketchbook but don't open it. The energy has shifted now, moved from art to architecture, from self-expression to combat readiness.

They want round two, I've been helping and working behind the scenes but this meeting was exactly what they needed to hear and see.

Good.

Because I didn't throw a match into that room just to watch it flicker.

I came to see who would stay when the fire caught.

I do not move right away.

The call ends, and the silence folds back into the house. It is not restful. It is aware. The kind of quiet that watches you instead of comforting you. It wraps around me like heat in the walls after a fire has passed through. Nothing is burning now, but everything knows it could be again.

I rise slowly. Not because I am uncertain, but because momentum deserves intention.

The hallway feels longer this time. My steps are light but grounded. I press my palm to the bedroom door and breathe once before I push it open.

Light cuts through the blinds in clean silver strips, casting long shadows across the floor. I cross the room and open the closet. No indecision. No reaching for something that softens or fades into the background.

I choose slate blue. A blouse with structure and silence sewn into the seams. The fabric has shape. It remembers its purpose. I pair it with sharp black pants, pressed to precision. These clothes do not ask for approval. They do not smile at first. They exist to hold space.

In the mirror, I pull my hair back. High. Clean. Tight enough to tell the truth. Each motion is a removal of distraction. A shedding of the impulse to charm or cushion. I reach for minimal makeup. Concealer to erase the fatigue. Mascara to sharpen the line of my stare. A touch of color on the mouth, not for softness, but for control.

I take one last look in the mirror. No corrections. No second guesses. I know exactly who is staring back at me.

This is not performance.

This is intention sharpened into presence.

I walk back through the hallway with calm, unbroken steps. The house no longer feels like a sanctuary. It feels like a pause. A holding place I have outgrown.

My hand closes around the front door handle just as my phone vibrates in my pocket.

The sound is muffled, but I already know.

I pull it out anyway. Let the screen light up in my hand.

JP.

No text. No voicemail. Just his name glowing back at me, full of silence and timing and all the things he still has not figured out how to say.

I stare at it for one beat longer than I need to. Then I press the screen dark and slide it back into my pocket without a word.

If he wants to speak, he'll have to catch up.

Because I am not answering anyone who shows up late to the fire.

I step outside and lock the door behind me.

And when I turn toward the day, I am no longer holding the heat back.

I am carrying it in both hands.

Chapter 16
Jenna & JP

Jenna

The hallway smells of chlorine, old sweat, and the kind of heavy-duty cleaner that never quite hides either. The floor tiles are dull from years of traffic; their grout darkened to a shade that will never see white again. Fluorescent lights buzz faintly overhead, their glow too sharp against walls painted in an uninspired beige. Two framed jerseys hang crooked. A baseboard is split where something hit it hard and stayed that way.

I notice everything, but none of it matters.

The only sound is the steady click of my heels, slow and deliberate, each step placed with intention. I keep my shoulders back and my gaze forward. I am not here to blend in. I am not here to warm a seat.

The receptionist glances up from her monitor. Her eyes flicker in recognition before she nods toward the stairs. "They're waiting for you upstairs."

Good. Let them wait.

The staircase groans under my measured pace. My fingertips trace the cool metal of the handrail for one brief moment. The air shifts as I climb, thinning the way it does before you step into altitude. It's quiet, expectant, heavier with what might happen next.

At the top, I stop.

Through the glass walls of the conference room, I see them. Mike sits near the head of the table, posture casual but eyes sharp. Two coaches, one jotting notes in a legal pad, the other with a white coffee cup cradled between both hands. Three players, arms crossed, their expressions caught between guarded interest and mild challenge.

And at the far end of the table, leaning forward just enough to signal attention without invitation, is JP.

I do not pause for him.

I press my palm to the glass. It is cool against my skin. I push the door open. The hinges release a slow, deliberate groan.

I let the sound travel across the room before I step inside.

No one speaks. Not yet.

The door closes behind me with a click that lands like a gavel. I cross to the table and set my folder down in the exact space I've chosen. The weight of it is small, but the sound carries. My hands rest lightly on the edges.

Only then do I lift my eyes.

I meet every face in the room before I speak.

"I understand there were questions."

JP

I knew she would come.

I told myself I was ready for it. I wasn't.

From the moment her footsteps echoed up the stairs, the air in the room changed. Conversations thinned. Even the players, who live to test boundaries, straightened in their seats.

And then she was here.

The glass door opened, and she walked in with the kind of composure that does not need speed or force to announce itself. The slate-blue blouse, the sharp line of her shoulders, the absence of even a glance in my direction — all of it said the same thing.

She is not here to be received.

She is here to take.

She placed her folder on the table like it was a fact, not a gesture. And then she spoke, each word clean, unhurried, landing exactly where she meant it to.

"I understand there were questions."

The air held still for a heartbeat.

And in that stillness, I felt the same pull I felt last night when she kissed me like there was nothing left to lose, only something to claim.

She hadn't answered my call. She didn't need to.

Because this was her answer.

Jenna

"I understand there were questions," I say, my voice carrying the even weight of someone who already knows the answers.

Mike leans forward in his chair, fingers laced loosely on the table. "We wanted to go over a few things from your proposal. Get some clarity."

The corner of my mouth doesn't move. "Clarity is not the problem here. Alignment is."

That lands. Even the coffee cup freezes halfway to the coach's mouth.

One of the players, the one sitting slightly forward like he's ready to challenge, speaks next. "So you're saying we're not on the same page?"

"I am saying," I answer, looking directly at him, "that some of you aren't reading the book."

His jaw tightens, but he doesn't look away.

I shift my gaze to the group at large. "You asked me here to explain a vision you already saw in black and white. If you didn't believe it then, you won't believe it now. So the real question is whether you're here to protect what you've always done or to build what you say you want."

No one rushes to respond.

The hum of the overhead lights fills the silence. I let it stay.

"You can debate colors, logos, the order of bullet points on a slide. That's cosmetic. What you can't fake is trust. What you can't brand your way out of is a locker room that's split in three directions. And what you can't afford to ignore is the fact that the public already knows."

I lean forward, resting my hands lightly on the folder in front of me. My voice lowers just enough that they have to lean in to hear it.

"I was not brought here to keep you comfortable. I was brought here to make sure you survive. If that makes me unpopular, good. Comfort doesn't win games. Comfort doesn't fill seats. And comfort doesn't make people believe in you again."

The player who spoke first shifts in his chair. Mike studies me like he's taking in the precise temperature of the fire.

I sit back. "So, let's save time. If what you really want is a new paint job on the same house, tell me now and I'll leave. But if you're ready to rebuild the foundation, then ask your questions and be ready for answers you might not like."

No one moves. No one speaks. The weight of my last words settles over the table like smoke that refuses to clear.

Then Benji shifts in his chair.

He's been quiet until now, lounging with one ankle hooked over his knee, looking for all the world like this is just another Tuesday. His grin is lazy. His eyes are not.

"Well," he says, tapping a pen against his palm, "at least we know she's not here to braid friendship bracelets and talk about team spirit."

A couple of the player's smirk. One even laughs under his breath.

Benji leans forward, warming to his own comment. "Look, I'm saying that as a compliment. She's not sugarcoating it. She's telling you what you need to hear, whether you like it or not."

It could have been fine. It should have landed as support.

But the way he says *friendship bracelets* hangs in the air just long enough for one of the coaches, the one with the coffee cup to tilt his head and slide right into the opening.

"So what I'm hearing," one of the coaches says smoothly, "is that this is more of a motivational pep talk than a structural plan. And motivation is great, but without actionable details, it's just a speech."

Benji opens his mouth to counter, but the damage is already done. The smirks from a moment ago have shifted into something else entirely like curiosity, maybe even the first flicker of challenge.

I watch the exchange without moving.

Benji meant to throw me a line. Instead, he handed them the rope.

The coffee cup coach leans back, clearly pleased with himself. "Without actionable details, it is just a speech," he says, looking down the table for agreement.

I meet his gaze. "The plan is in the proposal you already received. If you could not find the action in it, then the problem is either in your reading or in your commitment. Which one are we discussing today?"

A ripple moves through the table. It is not laughter. Not yet. Just awareness.

The coach starts to reply, but JP shifts forward in his chair, leaning toward the center of the table.

"All right, what she is saying," he begins.

"It does not need a translator," I say, my eyes still on the coach. My tone does not rise, but it carries enough weight to stop JP mid-breath.

I do not look at him. I do not offer him the courtesy of shared ground. The room is mine, and I have no intention of handing it over.

"What I am saying," I continue, "is that leadership that needs to be hand-held to understand a structural overhaul should reconsider whether they should be leading it. This is not a feel-good initiative. This is an operation to stabilize a fractured identity. If that sounds like a pep talk to you, then you should ask yourself why accountability sounds like inspiration."

The coach blinks once, his grip tightening on the coffee cup. The players shift in their seats, but no one laughs now.

The silence that follows is heavy and complete. It belongs entirely to me.

The silence stretches. It is not awkward. It is pressure. And pressure always forces someone to break.

It is the older of the two coaches who leans forward, folding his hands on the table. His voice is calm in the way people sound when they believe calm makes them untouchable.

"Ms. Monroe, we appreciate your... perspective," he says. "But in the end, this organization has a long history. Change here is not a matter of throwing out what came before and starting over. It is about respecting what was built while making adjustments. The identity you are suggesting feels... aggressive. And frankly, risky."

I hold his gaze. "Risky compared to what?"

He hesitates. "Compared to stability."

"Stability," I repeat, letting the word rest on my tongue for a moment before I set it down in the center of the table. "Do you know what stability looks like from the outside right now? It looks like empty seats. It looks like sponsors are hesitating to renew. It looks like a brand coasting on nostalgia while the competition is carving out your future."

I lean forward. My hands rest lightly on the folder in front of me, not as a shield, but as an anchor.

"Stability is a word people use when they are afraid to admit they have stopped growing. You call it respect for the past. I call it hiding behind it. You call it tradition. I call it fear. And fear will not save you when the people you serve start to believe you have nothing left to offer."

The room has gone still.

I let the stillness deepen before I finish.

"I am not here to dismantle what you built. I am here to make sure it does not collapse under the weight of its own comfort. You can keep your stability and watch everything you care about fade in slow motion. Or you can say yes to what I am putting in front of you and see what it feels like to win with both the past and the future on your side."

No one speaks.

Not the coaches. Not the players. Not even JP.

Mike finally nods once, his voice low. "Yes."

It is the only answer in the room.

Chapter 17

JP

It starts with a name on my lips before I even know I am saying it.

Jenna.

Practice ends just after five-thirty. Outside, the light is already slipping away, the sky a layered wash of steel gray and pale gold. It is the kind of evening that reminds you winter is close enough to taste. The cold has a sharper edge now. It gets into your lungs when you breathe and lingers there.

I know where she goes when she needs space. I have known for weeks, maybe longer, but I have never followed.

Not until now.

The truck hums along the back road out of town, past bare fields and the last clusters of stubborn oak leaves still clinging to their branches. The old Willow Cove sign flashes by, weatherworn and leaning, and the road narrows into gravel. I slow down. The tires crunch over frost-hardened stones, and the air spilling in through the cracked window is cold enough to bite.

I park in the pull-off by the trailhead. The lake is still a ten-minute walk from here. You don't end up there by accident. You have to choose it.

The path winds between trees stripped to bone, their branches black against the fading sky. Leaves crackle under my boots, dry and brittle, and the only other sound is the wind moving through the tree line. The air smells of pine and the metallic tang that comes before snow.

When the trail opens, the lake appears like a piece of glass dropped into the forest. Dark, still, and holding the last traces of light on its surface. The dock stretches out over the water, its boards silvered by frost and age.

She is there.

Jenna sits at the very edge, her bare feet skimming just above the water. A worn cardigan is wrapped around her, the sleeves pulled over her hands. The sketchbook beside her lies open, the pages lifting in the cold breeze. She does not look back when I step onto the dock, but the wood groans under my weight, and I know she hears me.

I stop a few feet behind her. I have been here before, almost in this same spot, almost in this same light. But I did not stay then. I did not close the distance.

I do now.

She does not look up. The pencil in her hand moves across the page in quiet, deliberate strokes, shaping something I cannot see from here.

"You finally decided to find me," she says. Her voice is even, without accusation, but it lands like a statement that expects an answer.

The tip of her pencil lifts for a moment before gliding back down. She does not turn. She does not slow.

"You always knew where I was, JP."

It is not a question.

I step closer, the boards creaking under my weight. The air between us carries the cold off the water, and I can see the pale cloud of my breath when I let it out.

"I did," I say. "But knowing isn't the same as showing up."

The pencil keeps moving.

"And I knew I should be here." I say slowly.

"Yet you weren't."

"No," I say. "I wasn't."

She tilts her head slightly, eyes still on her work. "And now?"

"I am."

The answer feels too small for what I mean, so I step closer. The space between us narrows to just a few boards. The dock shifts under the added weight.

Her pencil pauses for a heartbeat before continuing, as if my presence is nothing more than another detail to work around. "Because?"

"Because I don't want to leave you wondering again."

This time, the pencil stills completely for a brief moment.

Then the pencil moves in a final, deliberate line. Then she lifts it from the page and studies her work for a moment, her expression unreadable. Without showing it to me, she turns the sketchbook toward herself and folds it closed. Her hand rests lightly on the cover, holding it there.

I step forward until I'm beside her at the edge of the dock. The lake stretches out in front of us, dark and still, reflecting the last traces of fading light. My hands find my pockets, partly for warmth, partly to stop them from reaching for her before I have the right.

"I should have been here before now," I say.

Her gaze stays on the water.

"I should have been here when it was hard. When you didn't say you needed me but you still did. I kept telling myself that keeping my distance was about respect, about not making a mess of what we had."

The air bites against my skin, but I do not step back.

"It wasn't respectful. It was fear. Fear of not being enough. Fear of losing you before I had the chance to get it right."

She says nothing. The silence is heavier with her so close, but I hold it.

"I'm here now because I don't want to watch from a distance anymore," I continue. "And I won't let you sit on this dock wondering if I'm coming back."

Her fingers tap once against the closed sketchbook, but she doesn't look at me.

Without looking at me, she says, "And how long until you leave again?"

The words are soft, almost conversational, but they land like a stone dropped in deep water. There is no edge in her tone, only the kind of steadiness that makes the truth impossible to dodge.

I turn my head toward her, but she keeps her eyes on the lake.

"I'm not leaving," I say.

"You've said that before."

"Not like this." I step just a fraction closer, enough that I can see the pale cloud of her breath in the cold air. "I know what it costs when I disappear. I'm done making you pay that price. If I'm not ready to stay, then I shouldn't be here at all. And I am here."

The lake holds our reflections in fragments, her hair dark against the water, my shoulders drawn tight and I know this is the only moment that matters.

"I'm asking for the chance to prove it," I finish. "Every day, in small ways, until you don't have to ask me this question again."

Her hand tightens slightly on the sketchbook, and for the first time since I stepped onto the dock, I think she might let me see what she's been holding.

Jenna finishes the drawing in a few last, deliberate strokes. She studies it for a moment without showing me, then closes the sketchbook. Without a word, she sets it down on the bench beside me.

Straightening, she walks past, her shoulder brushing mine as she moves toward the far edge of the dock. The boards shift under her weight, the sound carrying in the still air. She stops at the end, hands loose at her sides, and stares down at the dark water below.

Her voice comes steady, carried back to me without her turning around. "Open it to the last page."

I pick up the sketchbook. The paper feels warm from her hands as I flip to the very end.

There she is. Drawn standing in front of me, her back against my chest. My arms are wrapped around her waist, my chin resting lightly on her shoulder. In the sketch, her head tilts slightly toward mine, her eyes closed, her mouth softened into the faintest curve. We are both facing forward, toward something I cannot see in the drawing, but the way she leans into me leaves no question that I am meant to be there.

I look from the image to her figure at the edge of the dock, still watching the water, and I feel the space between us in a way that makes me want to close it.

I keep my eyes on her as I rise from the bench. The sketchbook stays in my hand, but I no longer need to look at it. Every line is already etched into my mind.

The boards groan softly under my steps. She doesn't turn when I stop behind her. The wind off the lake brushes past us, carrying the faint scent of pine and cold water.

I slide my arms around her waist. She exhales, just enough for me to feel it under my hands. My chin finds the curve of her shoulder, exactly as she had drawn it.

For a moment, neither of us moves. The water below shifts and catches the fading light, and the reflection of the two of us ripples on its surface.

I do not speak. I do not promise. I just hold her, knowing that sometimes the only answer that matters is presence.

She leans back into me, and the space between the sketch and this moment disappears.

Epilogue

Jenna

One year later.

The light in the old lighthouse hits differently in the fall. It comes in low and warm, softened by the shorter days, and stretches across the tall windows like it has all the time in the world. It catches on the edges of my sketches and the corners of fabric swatches pinned in uneven rows along the wall. The air smells faintly of cedar from the floorboards, salt from the harbor below, and the coffee cooling in a mug beside my drafting table.

The space hums with quiet activity. My activity, there are projects in every stage of becoming scattered across the room with fresh pencil lines on tracing paper, swatches laid in careful stacks, measuring tape coiled beside a jar of brushes. It is still messy. Still chaotic. But it is the kind of chaos I can hold in my hands. The kind that reminds me this is mine.

Outside, the sea folds itself over the rocks, steady and unhurried. The sound carries up the hill in the same way it did the first day I unlocked this place. From somewhere farther down the slope comes the hum of the Willow Bean Café. Every now and then a door opens and laughter escapes, rising up with the crisp October air.

I pause with a pencil in my hand, leaning over the sketch I have been working on for the last hour. The lines are clean, purposeful. I let the moment settle in my chest the way the light settles across the desk. This is not just work. It is a life built in the open, with both feet planted and no door half-closed.

Footsteps sound in the hallway outside the studio, slow and familiar against the old wood. I do not look up right away. I finish the line I am working on before glancing toward the open doorway.

JP is there, framed by the late afternoon light from the stairwell window. His jacket is unzipped, his hair a little windblown from the walk up the hill. There is a faint streak of dust across his sleeve that tells me he has been at the rink, probably working with the kids again.

"You're missing the chaos at The Willow Bean," he says.

I set the pencil down and smile. "I have my own chaos here."

He steps inside, the boards creaking under his weight, and comes to stand behind me. His hand rests lightly on my shoulder before he bends to press a kiss to the side of my head. He smells of cold air and the faint metallic tang of the rink, layered over something warmer that is his alone.

His eyes find the wall in front of my desk. There, pinned with a silver clip, is the sketch I finished last night with an abstract mix of color and line, with three words hand-lettered beneath it in bold charcoal strokes.

Still chaotic. Still loved. Still here.

He reads them once, then again. The quiet between us feels full.

"You stayed," he says, his voice low.

I turn to look up at him. "So did you."

The answer seems to be enough for both of us. He threads his fingers through mine and gives a gentle squeeze, the kind of silent invitation I have learned to recognize.

The Willow Bean is warm enough that my glasses fog slightly as I step inside. The air is rich with the scent of cinnamon, baked bread, and freshly ground coffee. Conversation hums at every table, layered with the soft clink of mugs against saucers and the occasional burst of laughter.

Maisie spots us first. She is behind the counter with Miss Edie, arranging a tray of cookies into careful spirals. Her hair is tucked under a knit cap that sits slightly askew, and she is concentrating so hard on getting the pattern right that Miss Edie's smile widens with each adjustment.

"You are late," Maisie announces, not even looking up from the tray as if she has been rehearsing the line.

"I did not know we had a time," I say, stepping closer.

"You always have a time," she replies, and then she looks up and hands me a cookie with both hands, like it is part of some official welcome ceremony.

Miss Edie shakes her head and slides a mug of coffee toward JP. "Do not mind her. She has been timing everyone who comes in since ten this morning."

Benji is leaning against the far end of the counter. He is in the middle of a story that has his audience of two older men from the hardware store laughing so hard one of them has to brace a hand on the counter. Benji pauses long enough to lift his chin toward us in greeting, then drops back into the story with a grin that tells me he knows exactly how to keep his crowd hooked.

The café feels alive. It is the kind of life that makes me want to stand still for a moment and watch it. The light streaming in through the windows glances off the framed prints along the wall. The menu board catches the eye with its bold lettering and bright chalk colors. The hand-painted sign above the counter still carries the brushstrokes I left there last winter. This is more than a café. It is a piece of what we built, a place where the air itself feels warmer because it has been shaped by familiar hands.

JP nudges my hand, and when I look at him, he tips his head toward the chalkboard near the counter. It is the one where the day's specials are written in a mixture of neat letters and quick scribbles. I already know what he wants me to do.

I step toward the chalkboard near the counter. It stands taller than me, the surface smudged with faint traces of past menus and notes. Miss Edie notices where I am headed and disappears under the counter for a moment before pressing a small box of chalk into my hands.

"Go ahead," she says, her voice soft but carrying over the hum of the room. "You always make it better."

I kneel slightly and clear a corner of the board with the small cloth she keeps tucked into the frame. The cloth smells faintly of lemons from whatever cleaner she used that morning. Around me, the café continues its rhythm with the hiss of the espresso machine, the clatter of plates in the dish tub, the low murmur of conversations that weave together into a steady hum.

JP stays a few feet away, leaning on the counter with his coffee in hand. His eyes follow every movement, but he does not say a word.

The black surface is cool beneath my fingertips as I begin to write. The chalk leaves a crisp white line that curves into the first letter, then another, each one looping into the next in my usual slow, deliberate script. My world narrows to the way the chalk feels as it moves, to the faint scrape it makes as it meets the board.

Still chaotic. Still loved. Still here.

When I finish the last curve, I pause with the chalk still in my hand, letting the words settle into the space. They stand out against the dark background, clean and sure.

I step back from the board and set the chalk in the small tray at its base. The words look right. They belong here.

Miss Edie comes out from behind the counter; her apron dusted with flour. She smooths the front of it with both hands before stopping in front of the board. Her eyes move slowly over the words, taking in every line.

After a long moment, she nods once. "That is the truth of this place," she says. Her voice is calm, but there is a softness beneath it. "And the truth of you. You have your roots in the right ground now, Jenna. And roots like that will hold, no matter what storms come."

The air in my chest feels tight.

JP steps closer until his shoulder rests against mine. His voice is low, meant only for me. "That is us."

I look at him, my smile small but certain. "That is us."

Miss Edie's gaze lingers on me a moment longer before she turns slightly toward JP. "You hold onto her, and she will hold onto you. That is how it works when you both choose to stay."

He nods, but I can feel in the way he looks at me that he already knows. He knows this is what it will be like from now on. Not perfect, not simple. Just steady. Just ours.

I turn back to the board. The chalk letters are simple, but they hold everything.

Still chaotic. Still loved. Still here.

Through the window, tiny rain drops start to fall coating the town under the late afternoon light. Inside, the people I love are close enough to touch, and the air is warm with belonging.

This time, it was never about the storm. It was about what came after.

Together, we are still here. And this time, that is all it takes.

JP's gaze stays on me as the words sink in. He knows with absolute certainty that this will be our life. No matter what comes, no matter what changes, I will be here and so will he. And for the first time, forever does not feel like a promise. It feels like the truth.

The End.

Check These Out

Whispers of Spring: A Small Town Love at First Sight Sweet Romance

Spring awakens new love in this charming, small-town tale.

Summer's Embrace: A Small Town Second Chance Sweet Romance

Feel the warmth of summer and the magic of rekindled love.